The story of his son's murder had now faded from the front page, but Farris was condemned to remember. And so his dreams were filled with terrifying images of his son's last moments. At three o'clock in the morning he would awaken and in his pajamas stand by the window smoking and drinking whiskey. At such times he also considered the years that lay ahead of him. And so at eleven-thirty on this cloudy Friday he stood in his kitchen finishing his third drink of the day....

". . . unforgettable characters . . . brutal . . . anguished
. . . *Chicago Tribune*

"*Final Things* . . . its impact is formidable."
Kansas City Star

"*Final Things* works!" *Best Sellers*

FINAL THINGS

RICHARD B. WRIGHT

ace books
A Division of Charter Communications Inc.
A GROSSET & DUNLAP COMPANY
51 Madison Avenue
New York, New York 10010

FINAL THINGS

Copyright © 1980 by Richard B. Wright

All rights reserved. No part of this book may be reproduced in any form or by any means, except for the inclusion of brief quotations in a review, without permission in writing from the publisher.

All characters in this book are fictitious. Any resemblance to actual persons, living or dead, is purely coincidental.

An ACE Book,
by arrangement with E.P. Dutton Publishing Co., Inc.

First ACE Printing: April 1982

2 4 6 8 0 9 7 5 3 1
Manufactured in the United States of America

To Phyllis

Into many a green valley
 Drifts the appalling snow

> W.H. AUDEN

PART ONE

CHAPTER ONE

When, after an hour, Farris's twelve-year-old son did not return to the apartment, the man began to worry. He had been watching TV football and drinking canned beer, but now he turned off the set and walked to his front window. He lived in a four-story apartment building called the Del Monte Arms on the east side of Sherbourne Street just north of Carlton. It was now four o'clock and the mild gray November afternoon was nearly over. Farris's apartment was on the second floor, and along the street under his window people carrying bags of groceries and liquor walked hurriedly toward rooming houses and small hotels. Automobiles moved easily through the light traffic. Standing there looking out over the street, Farris tried to gauge his anxiety. The boy had been gone for an hour, which wasn't that long. Twelve-year-old kids can be distracted by many things, and perhaps he was now looking at skin magazines in the variety store and had lost track of the time. On the other hand, Farris's stern and secretive son was usually very careful about time. When he went to the variety story for candy or soft drinks, he always returned within twenty-five minutes, at the most a half hour.

Farris considered phoning his ex-wife, but perhaps it was too early for that. Besides, Pat would not be happy to learn that the boy was loose in the neighborhood. It was one of her favorite criticisms of Farris's life. That and his drinking. To her he lived in an unsafe area populated by derelicts and perverts and criminals. And so she worried about Jonathan's Saturday visits to his father, even though Farris picked up his son and later delivered him to Prince Arthur Avenue. But Farris didn't find his neighborhood particularly unsafe. Anyway, where was safe? The world was a treacherous place whether you lived in downtown Toronto among strangers or in a farmhouse in Kansas among tornadoes. And so he had lived in this building with its flaking sand-colored paint since the collapse of his marriage over a year ago. He liked the area. It was lively and convenient and inexpensive. The sirens from the ambulances going to the hospital a couple of blocks away were a nuisance, but you got used to them. And Farris liked too the small park at the corner with its glass conservatory where you could step into thick tropical heat on a February afternoon. Here were the derelicts Pat liked to talk about when discussing safety. But to Farris they were mostly harmless, defeated men who looked either unhappy or ill in their large overcoats and sockless shoes. In the afternoons they slept on the grass or sat on the benches eating buns from paper bags. With winter approaching, they would move farther south along the street to the men's hostels. Farris wanted his son to see people like that. The boy was mostly surrounded by wealth. But here he could see men and women who were imperfect or unlucky; people who lived in one room and shared a kitchen and got drunk and violent on Saturday nights.

And Jonathan appeared to enjoy it. He particularly looked forward to his walk to the variety store a couple of blocks away. Once Farris had gone along, but that was not a success. Jonathan was irritable and abstracted, and later Farris realized that his son wished to be alone, if only for a little while. When Farris thought more about it he understood. During the week Jonathan attended Germanfield Academy, a boys' boarding school sixty miles away, and he complained bitterly about the lack of privacy there. Jonathan was plaintive by nature, but Farris was sympathetic. As a kid he wouldn't have liked the place either. He didn't like it when he visited the school in September. But Jonathan loathed the school entirely and that was understandable. He was a loner and he hated the compulsory sports. He said he had no friends and his roommates laughed at him because he kept tropical fish, a gift from his grandfather. The kid was unhappy and Farris was unhappy for him. He would gladly have driven down to Germanfield and packed the boy's bags, but Pat wouldn't hear of it. To her that was quitting. Jonathan had only been at Germanfield a few weeks; he hadn't given the school a chance. It was an excellent place with devoted teachers, etc., etc. After one of his tantrums, she finally made him promise to try it until Christmas. But as he told his father, "I don't care what you or Mother do to me. I'm not staying in that place after Christmas. I'll run away." His mother was also sending him to a psychiatrist, a man Farris had met only once and neither liked nor trusted.

Being old-fashioned, Farris grieved over his ruined marriage and the loss of his beautiful wife, whom he still loved. Toward his handsome and surly son he felt a protective love and only wished the boy were happier. Yet often when they were together, each felt tense and wary. Today, for instance, Farris had suggested they go to a movie, but the boy only shrugged. Instead he sat on the sofa thumbing through old *National Geographics,* his jaw slack and the dark hair falling across his brow. He was bored and his silence seemed like a reproach. It said that Farris had somehow contrived to spoil the shape and color of the afternoon. When he was like this, Jonathan annoyed his father. To soothe his irritation, Farris drank a few cans of beer, though he felt more like whiskey. But he was childishly eager to remind Jonathan that his father was no longer a drunk. When it came time for the boy to walk to the variety store, Farris was almost glad to see him go. He then settled down to the football game. In a way this was business. A former newspaperman, Farris was now a magazine writer who specialized in sports stories. Over the last dozen years or so he had written scores of articles on hockey players and pool sharks and prizefighters. Along the way he had published a novel, a minor work now largely forgotten. It was written in a Gloucestershire village during the happiest year of an unhappy life. For twenty years Farris had been a heavy drinker, but for the past several months he had been trying to stay sober. It was difficult and at times impossible, for at forty-three Farris felt somehow imperiled by life. There were periods when his concentration was bad and weeks when he couldn't put two sentences together. At nights he often lay awake and worried about surviving.

Now, however, he worried about his son. Perhaps he shouldn't have let the boy go by himself to the variety store. Yet the kid was twelve years old and it had been the middle of the afternoon. There were children in the neighborhood who walked the streets every day. This wasn't some kind of slum jungle where zonked teenagers dropped bricks on your head or mugged you in broad daylight. And anyway, Jonathan would have been furious at the suggestion that he was not old enough to walk the street. So despite what Pat might think, Farris could not believe that it was especially dangerous. And his son was intelligent. He knew the old stories about not talking to strangers and not getting into cars. Yet Farris began to feel afraid; Jonathan was not back and he should have been. On his way out he stopped at Mrs. Farnsworth's apartment next door and asked her to watch for the boy. She was only too glad to help and said she would leave her door ajar in case Jonathan returned before his father. Mrs. Farnsworth was already half-drunk and regarded Farris sadly with her watery, alcoholic eyes. He smelled the gin on her and was deeply envious.

Outside, he walked quickly south toward Carlton, scanning both sides of the street. But in the variety store the owner, a young Greek, only shrugged at Farris's questions. The store was busy and the owner continued to fill a customer's bag. He told Farris that he saw dozens of kids every day, but took notice only of the ones who stole from him. In his kind of business you had to watch for that. As he talked, he rang up the customer's sale, and Farris felt like striking the man. How could he be so uncaring? Farris left the store sick with worry and rage. On the street again he asked passersby if they had seen a dark-haired boy in blue cords and Windbreaker. Some gave him looks of sympathy; others didn't understand his questions. They were immigrants and they thought Farris was asking them for money. Thus, with embarrassment, they stepped around him and hastened away. He walked east on Carlton, entering any store that sold candy or magazines. Finally, in one such store he bought cigarettes, yielding to an old habit he thought he'd kicked. Standing outside, he lit his first smoke in over a year and it left him feeling guilty and lightheaded. The sky was now emptied of color and along Carlton Street the lights blazed. In another hour it would be night, and Farris felt utterly bereft. When he walked into the darkening corner of Allan Gardens, he met only a few persons hurrying past on their way home. No one was now loitering in the small park. After all, he thought, it was nearly a November night.

It was past five o'clock when he returned to his apartment building, taking the stairs quickly and hoping that Jonathan would be waiting for him. The door to Mrs. Farnsworth's apartment was open on the chain and he could hear her television. But when he glanced in, he could see that she was alone. Now he would have to phone Pat, and it came to him in a spasm of hope that Jonathan might simply have returned to his mother's. He couldn't imagine why the boy would do such a thing without telling him, but who knew what went on in a twelve-year-old's mind. If indeed he was there, Farris vowed to go over and kick the boy's arse right in front of his mother and her handsome young Englishman, Peter Neville. Dreading this call and badly needing a drink, Farris dialed his wife's number. Peter Neville answered almost immediately. He recognized Farris's voice and called out to Pat. Neville's confident air vexed the writer, who suspected there was little to the man except good looks and energy. But he was a successful producer of educational TV programs. He was also ten years younger than Pat, and the thought of his wife loving someone who was only in his late twenties filled Farris with sour jealousy. Then his wife was on the line, and when Farris asked her if Jonathan had returned, he heard the sharp intake of breath and felt his own heart sinking. Pat's voice was crisp and cold. "No . . . why should he be here? You said you'd bring him back at the usual time. Where is he?" Farris counted slowly to five; he had involved his wife and this was now a serious matter. He spoke flatly. "I don't know. He went out to get some pop and chips a couple of hours ago and he hasn't come back."

Pat's voice rose slightly. "Hasn't come back? In two hours? Jesus Christ, Charlie, what have you been doing all this time?"

Farris reminded himself to be calm and patient. He concealed his sense of grievance. "Well, I went out looking. I walked around." She interrupted him. "What the hell is going on, Charlie? Did you two quarrel?"

"No . . . nothing like that. Look, we were sitting around reading. Then he went out for some chips and pop. To the variety store. It's only a couple of blocks away. It's routine. He does this all the time."

"Have you been drinking this afternoon?" she asked.

"No . . . not really. A couple of beers. That's it." Like small children, drunks were constantly suspected of mischief. And she didn't believe him. He could hear her voice wavering.

"Damn it, Charlie. Two hours? And in that crummy neighborhood? You let him go out by himself. This is the first time I've heard about that."

"Look, Pat. It was the middle of the afternoon. He always went for candy. He enjoyed going to the store. He's a sensible kid. He's twelve years old. He's not a baby anymore."

Farris wasn't certain, but he thought his wife might be weeping.

"He's not sensible. He's not relating to people at all. He's going through a period of stress. If you had paid more attention to what Dr. Toomey said, you'd understand your son a little better. But you were too busy calling Dr. Toomey a quack." And I haven't changed my mind, either, thought Farris. Toomey was a hearty little Irish fraud who tried to joke his way into your life with stories. Jonathan saw through him in ten minutes and regarded his sessions with the psychiatrist as a bad joke. He called Toomey the Leprechaun. Over the telephone he would inform Farris about these sessions. "Well, I've just had another hour with the Leprechaun, begorra. . . And say, did you hear about the fellah . . . this happened years ago in the west country. . ." Those malicious and funny imitations were the boy's only form of humor. Farris thought about this as he listened to his wife rebuke him. "Jonathan is not sensible. He is many things, Charlie, but sensible is not one of them. In many ways he is still a very little boy." Thanks to you and your father, Farris felt like saying, but didn't. She paused and then said viciously, "Goddamn you, Charlie. You should have taken better care of him." Now she was openly sobbing and he could hear Neville asking what was wrong.

Farris lit a cigarette with trembling fingers and listened to a siren noise winding through the streets. Intimations of tragedy gripped his heart. Then Peter Neville was speaking to him. "Charlie? This is Peter. Now, please don't be angry. I want to help. How long has Jonathan been gone?" Farris resented bitterly this precise and cool Oxford voice. After all, it wasn't Neville's son who was missing. Yet he knew that

Peter loved Pat very much and did his best with Jonathan, who did not like the man at all. Still, this was a family matter; it belonged to him and Pat, not her lover.

"Nearly two and a half hours now," said Farris irritably.

"Has he done this before?" asked Neville. "Stayed away for this length of time?"

Farris was piqued by the interrogation. "Who the fuck do you think you are, Neville? The fucking cops? Let me talk to Pat."

"Charlie, I'm only trying to help. Pat's very distressed."

"Distressed. Right. She's probably also upset. As I am. Now get off the fucking phone and let me talk to her."

Farris next heard Neville saying something to Pat. He was offering advice and Farris heard the word *police*. Outside his window it was now dark and he stood by the telephone feeling awkward and guilty. With each passing moment his life seemed diminished. The orderly scheme of things had been violated, and he realized that what he was now feeling was the first stage of panic. Pat was speaking to him now and her voice crackled like burning paper. "Now listen, Charlie. Jonathan has been acting very strange lately. He's been very depressed. Dr. Toomey has been worried about him. Surely you've noticed these moods of his." Farris hesitated. "Well, he's always been a moody kid. I'm a moody person. It runs in the family."

"I'm calling Dr. Toomey and I think we should now get in touch with the police."

"All right. Agreed. You or me?"

She flared with old anger. "Well, for God sakes,

Charlie, he was in *your* care. They'll want to talk to you first. Now phone them while I get in touch with Toomey."

"Sure. Listen, Pat." He wanted desperately to reassure her. "The kid maybe is down. It's possible. It's hard to tell sometimes with Jonathan. He's seldom a barrel of laughs, you know. But he didn't say much today, just yes please and no thanks. But he'll be okay. He probably just wanted to get away by himself for a bit. You know that goddamn boarding school doesn't give him any privacy. He's a private person. He might just have gone for a walk. Just to get away from people." His wife only sounded exasperated with him.

"Charlie? Have you looked outside? It's dark now. This city has over two million people. He could meet up with anyone."

Her voice caught on the last word. She was right, too, and Farris felt another spurt of fear deep in his bowels. He had never loved his wife more than at this moment. "Yeah. Well sure, but let's not let our imaginations get carried away. He has money. He wouldn't take any from me. He said he had a few bucks. Right now he's probably eating chips and having Coke in some restaurant. Maybe he's afraid to come back. . . ."

Her voice was almost dry now. She might have been dealing with a child who didn't understand the serious nature of all this. "Peter will stay here in case Jonathan turns up. I'm coming over there. I'm leaving immediately. Now phone the police." She paused and then said sadly, "Damn it, Charlie, why do you do these things to me?"

"What things?" asked Farris. But she had hung up on him.

* * *

In his small kitchen he took down the unopened bottle of Teacher's Highland Cream and poured two inches into a tumbler. He drank it straight off and felt the warmth spreading through his belly. Then he lit another cigarette and phoned the police.

CHAPTER TWO

They arrived five minutes later. Looking down, Farris watched the yellow patrol car stop below his window, its hazard lights blinking as the policemen climbed out. Farris pushed the buzzer to open the lobby door, and in a minute they were standing in his apartment with their caps off, two stolid young men who seemed to fill the small room. They listened respectfully while he gave them details, and one of them wrote everything carefully on a pad. Farris also gave them a picture, a recent school photograph in which Jonathan stared solemnly out at the world with thoughtful eyes. There was terrible pride and insolence in his face and Farris saw himself there. While they were talking, Pat arrived, hurrying through the doorway. She looked pale and furious and frightened. Casting aside her leather coat, she shook out her thick dark hair and stood by with her arms folded across her breasts, frowning at everyone. The two cops asked her some questions about Jonathan's schedule that morning and then they moved toward the door. Before leaving, one of them muttered something about this all being routine. Nine times out of ten the child has just run away and he comes home when he's cold and tired and hungry.

And since Jonathan had only five or six dollars, he couldn't go far. The bashful young policeman looked embarrassed saying all this, but Farris was grateful and thanked him. Pat had turned her back to them and said nothing. After they left, both Farris and his wife stood by the window and watched the policemen climb into the patrol car. Already a small crowd, mostly youngsters leaning on bikes, had gathered on the sidewalk.

The cops seemed to take forever to leave and Farris guessed they were radioing information across the city. His son was now the object of a police search, and Farris felt his own life pulled in the direction of larger, darker things. He wondered what Pat was thinking as she stood beside him gazing down at the street, absently leaning her brow against the glass. She looked stricken, and, watching her, Farris sensed the enormous loss and waste of his life. He lamented especially the terrible failure of their lives together. When he was alone, this small, drab place seemed right. But with his wife beside him, he felt only embarrassed and apologetic. Everything he had done wrong in his life seemed to surround him in the stale air of these rooms: his drunkenness, his long moody spells of inactivity, his affairs on out-of-town assignments; they were all here at the Del Monte Arms. And somehow he wanted to explain and make amends. Instead he only asked her if she wanted a drink. In refusing, she shook her head angrily. He could see she was fighting back tears and he warned himself to take heed. Yet in the kitchen he quickly drank another scotch. It tasted like nothing and he knew he could drink it all night. Then from the front room he heard Pat say softly, "Don't get drunk on me, Charlie. Not tonight, please!" In the kitchen Farris felt like the victim of a massive insult. How could she think he would get drunk tonight with his son missing?

He tried to sound offended when he called out to her, "I'm not getting drunk, Pat. Listen, he'll be all right. I think that cop was correct. The kid is upset over something. So he ran away to think a few things through. It probably happens hundreds of times every day in this city. All over the world, for that matter. He's nearly a teenager. Kids at Johnny's age get mixed up. They want to get off by themselves and sort things out. Jesus . . . I can understand that." He was talking too much, and when he went to the front room Pat turned to face him. Farris was aghast at her scornful look.

"Charlie! If anything's happened to him!"

Farris sat down heavily and stared at the rug. "He'll be all right, goddamn it." But he felt overwhelmed by her pessimism. Yet what the hell was he talking about? If you wanted positive thinking, you didn't come to Charlie Farris. Pat sat down opposite him, flinging her arm over the back of the sofa. In her roll-neck sweater and jeans she looked ten years younger. But when she spoke she sounded older. "You don't know him," she said.

"Who knows anybody?" said Farris bleakly.

"Look," she said, "you only see him on Saturday afternoons. He's just not himself. And he hasn't been for the past six months."

"Well, that's understandable," said Farris. He had never forgiven his wife for divorcing him. "He doesn't exactly have a normal home anymore."

Pat looked away. "Did he ever have a *normal* home, as you put it?"

Farris resented her sarcasm. "You know what I mean, goddamn it. The kid doesn't have a family anymore. He spends all week in that expensive fucking prison they call a school where he hasn't made any friends. . ."

Pat leaned forward and said patiently, "Charlie, the boy has made no friends since nursery school. According to Toomey, it's not in Jonathan's behavior pattern to be sociable."

"On the weekends," continued Farris, ignoring her, "he comes to the city and we shuttle him back and forth like somebody's pale little orphan cousin. The same thing happens on his holidays. A week here . . . a week there. We slice up his time like . . . like. . ." He was slapping the arm of the chair as he searched for a simile. Finally he gave up in disgust. "The only time he seemed happy was last summer at your father's cottage. I think Bill's the only person Johnny gives a damn about."

Pat now looked over at him in horror. "My God! What can I say to Dad? If anything happened to Jonathan it would kill him."

"Don't tell him anything," said Farris, "not a thing. Let's just take all this an hour at a time."

Pat sank her cheek into her fist and again looked out the window. "If I could talk to Toomey . . ." she said quietly.

"Did you call him?"

"His answering service said he was away for the weekend attending some conference in Philadelphia." She was clearly irked by this. And Farris reflected that it was like her to expect everyone to be available for service at a moment's notice. He said finally, "Well, so what? What can he say? What we need now are cops, not psychiatrists." She looked over at him.

"If you'd think about it for a minute, Charlie, you'd see. Maybe you'd understand. Over the past few weeks Toomey has come to know him a helluva lot better than either of us. Maybe, just maybe, he could give us some idea of Jonathan's behavior pattern."

Behavior pattern. Right. Farris rolled his eyes and looked at the ceiling with irritation. "I don't know why you put such faith in those people, Pat. Now, this Toomey is a droll little character, I give you that. All his paddy-whackery must be charming if you like that sort of thing. One of the few things Johnny *has* told me over the past weeks is how comical these sessions with Toomey are. The kid is sharp enough, thank God, to see that a lot of this stuff is a racket. Tell me all about your childhood and what nasty people your parents are. Well, I could have told him that. Hell, I *have* told him that. Ask me about *my* parents sometime. I am a son of a bitch. I've made lots of mistakes. I screwed up our marriage. With a little help from you, of course. And I'm sorry. I'm fucking sorry. I've told all this to my son. It doesn't really change anything, does it? So here we are..." He had raised his hands in a gesture of hopelessness, but now they dropped to his knees. He felt a certain perverse satisfaction in reviving all this. They had been through it dozens of times.

"You didn't pay enough attention to him, Charlie," she said. "You were too self-absorbed."

That was true, but like most things only up to a point. He fiercely loved his son. The times he had sat by the bed watching the boy sleep, noting the lift and fall of the narrow chest. And that year in England when he had been working on the novel. How happy they had been! In the afternoons he carried the child on his shoulders around the edges of the fields of grain and into the long sloping pasture where heavy black-and-white cows lay under the trees. And as he walked, he had said to himself over and over, "This is good. How happy I am! I must cherish this." And now when he thought about it, a deep sense of wonder and peace passed through him.

But yes, she was right; he had been a loving but bad father. He had been indifferent and secretive when trying to meet a deadline. When the work wasn't going well he was worse, sullenly sipping beer and watching daytime TV. Wanting only to be left alone. How could you expect a kid to understand that? But the year in England was like a poultice on such wounds in his memory. On bad nights he went to sleep retracing walks through summer evenings to the local pub. Johnny was safe in the care of a neighbor, and he and Pat drank beer and ate fish and chips at the King's Head. Now he looked across at his former wife. She had got up and was standing again by the window. "Do you remember that year in England, Pat?" he asked. "Christ, that was a good year. That was absolutely the best year of my life. Do you remember that walk we used to take on Friday nights to the pub? And the people? Jesus, I really liked some of those people. And I worked well there, too. Do you ever think about that year?"

"Yes," she said, "sometimes."

"But not often, right?" said Farris. It annoyed him to think that she did not place the same value as he did on that year.

"No," she said, "not often." It was left there and he swallowed his anger like medicine.

"Are you sure you don't want a drink?" he asked after a moment. "No," she said. Farris guessed she had taken a Valium after he phoned her. During the last few months of their marriage Pat secretly used Valium. She hid them in a dresser beneath her underwear, too proud to admit she couldn't handle the stress. Pat then startled him by asking for a cigarette. She hadn't smoked in years; he clearly remembered when she quit. That was the year she ate only yogurt and granola for months. "Are you sure?" he asked.

"It's all right. Just give me one, please." He lit it for her and she deeply inhaled as she sat down. In the pallid light of the room she looked ill and mildly disgusted with herself.

"How about some coffee?" asked Farris.

"Yes. All right," she said, "make some coffee. What time is it? This goddamn watch has stopped." She shook her wrist furiously and placed the watch next to her ear. "Two hundred and fifty dollars and the fucking thing has stopped." The watch was a gold-plated digital affair, thin as a wafer, a birthday present from Neville, according to Jonathan, who reported to his father on all gifts offered and received. To Farris his son was maddeningly obsessed with consumer goods and could give you expert advice on the value of stereos or water skis or sports cars.

"It's nearly seven o'clock," said Farris from the kitchen. Pat smoked her cigarette greedily; the smoke billowed from her mouth as she spoke. "So he's been gone now what? About four hours?"

"Yes," said Farris warily, "about four hours. That's right." He laid out the cups with elaborate care and listened to the coils heating in the electric kettle. Soon the water was steaming and he spooned instant coffee into the cups, pouring the boiling water over the brown powder. This homely task seemed to calm him, but then the phone interrupted, and he grabbed for the receiver on the wall. "Yes? Hello?"

"Hello, Charlie. Is there any news?" It was Peter Neville.

"No," said Farris.

"Nothing there, I suppose. He hasn't turned up?"

"Obviously not," said Farris coldly. Neither of them spoke for a moment, and then Farris asked him if he wanted to speak to Pat.

"Yes, Charlie. If it isn't too much trouble. Please."

If it isn't too much trouble, thought Farris. *Christ.* Where do people learn to use such expressions? In British public schools, he supposed. Pat had stubbed out her cigarette and now walked to the phone. Farris handed her the receiver and then brought her the coffee, carefully laying his cigarettes and matches alongside. He then poured a generous shot of whiskey into his coffee and resumed his vigil by the window, trying not to listen. In any case, there wasn't much to hear; Neville was doing most of the talking. After a minute Pat hung up and came back into the front room. She seemed more restive than before.

"Do you still honestly think Jonathan is sitting in some restaurant drinking Coke and afraid to come home?"

"It's certainly possible," said Farris.

"Well, I don't," she said. "I think something dreadful has happened." She was smoking again and looking away from him, hugging her elbows. She looked so distraught he could have wept. She herself was close to tears as he walked across to her. "Listen, Pat, I'm sorry. I should never have let the kid out of my sight. Maybe I treated him too much as a grown-up. At times he seemed so damned adult. Listen, believe me, if anything's happened to him, I'll never forgive myself. But look, it's only a few hours. Christ, maybe Johnny's decided that he's had it with that snotty private school. He didn't like the place. You know that."

"But if he didn't like it," she insisted, "it's because he didn't give it a chance. He was only there a couple of months. We'd have taken him out at Christmas if he didn't adapt. We told him that. Only a few more weeks." Farris resented her use of the word *we*. She obviously meant Neville and herself.

"All right," said Farris, "but the wait for Christmas can be a lifetime for an unhappy twelve-year-old. So he's miserable at the school all week. And then on the weekends, what? A Saturday-morning session with a stage Irishman and then the shuttle service between you and me. He gets fed up. And who can blame him? So he's determined to try it on his own. A mad idea for a twelve-year-old, but an idea anyway. Maybe he's got it in his head to hitchhike West and be a cowboy or something."

Pat shook her head violently. "Jonathan may be difficult, Charlie, but he's not stupid. He'd never start hitchhiking in the middle of a November afternoon. It would take him an hour to get out of the city. Then it would be nearly dark. Winter will soon be here, Charlie." The tears had started up in her eyes.

"I know that," said Farris gruffly. He himself was not far from tears.

"He only had a few dollars," she continued. "Your theory just doesn't make any sense at all."

Farris turned from her in anger. "All right, it doesn't make any fucking sense. If you say so. . . But I was only trying to be a little fucking optimistic. That's all."

Pat hastily stubbed out her cigarette. "It's no use. I can't stay here. Don't take offense, Charlie, but this goddamn place depresses me. I don't know why you insist on living here. If you'd pull yourself together and get some assignments and move into a decent neighborhood. I haven't seen your name on an article in months."

"I didn't think you were still looking."

"Oh, don't get me wrong, I'm not. I'd just like to see you move so that when our son visits you he doesn't have to come to this desperate place."

"I like it here," said Farris stubbornly, "and it may surprise you to learn that Jonathan does, too."

"Christ," she said. These familiar scoldings. Farris wondered how the Englishman coped with them. Farris had lived with them for a dozen years. Once in the middle of an argument he had belted her, but she still kept talking through a swollen mouth. She never knew when to quit.

"I don't know how anyone can like it," she said. "These musty old apartment buildings. An old folks' home up the street. A couple of fleabag hotels. And that Allan Gardens right around the corner. Every bum and pervert and wino in the country passes through there. It's a helluva place to bring a twelve-year-old to and you know it." It was out now; she would never forgive him if anything happened to Jonathan. But then he wasn't sure he could ever forgive himself. Farris drained his doctored coffee and tried to sound calm.

"Pat, there are plenty of twelve-year-old kids living around here. They survive. Not everybody can afford to live on Prince Arthur Avenue or attend a private school."

At the door she was buckling her leather coat and knotting the strap. "Well, you can afford better than this. Let's just pray that nothing's happened."

"Don't worry. He'll be all right." Farris walked over to her. "This is probably just a little adventure he's pulling off. Lots of kids run away." It was possible, wasn't it? The kid had run away and was hitching West to be a cowboy. It takes a lot of balls to do something like that at twelve years old. This time next year they'd laugh about it.

"I'll talk to you later, Charlie," she said. For a moment it was like old times when he would be leaving for an assignment out of town and neither wanted to part. In those days they embraced ardently and whispered promises to each other. Now an old habit almost made them do it again. But there had been too much bitterness, and so she turned and walked to the elevator. A moment later Farris watched her climb into her gray Mercedes. She didn't look up. Then the car pulled away, smoothly heading north toward Bloor Street.

When she had gone, Farris wondered whether he should have another drink but decided against it. Instead he phoned the police and asked for Missing Persons. A polite man told him that all units were alerted. So far there was no sign of the boy, but that was not unusual. It was night and Toronto was a big city. Was there anything Farris could do? The man was kind but firm. They had all the information they needed for the moment. Farris and his wife had been very cooperative and the boy's picture was helpful. If Jonathan didn't turn up by morning, a couple of detectives would be around for more detailed information. Right now there was nothing else they could tell him. The officer advised Farris to phone his family doctor and arrange to have a mild tranquilizer delivered; it's what most people did in the circumstances. Farris hung up the phone. He didn't have a family doctor.

Filled with foreboding, he paced off his rooms, moving from his small yellow kitchen to the living room with its brown corduroy sofa and chair and then to his bedroom, which doubled as a workroom. Looking out the side window to the next building, he saw a man watching the hockey game, the blurred figures shifting across the Technicolor screen. And here in this bedroom were his books and his desk with its portable Underwood and the goose-necked writing lamp. Tools of his trade. Now and then he still received a fan letter, the envelope forwarded by a stranger at his publisher's.

Time passed slowly when your heart was weighted with dread, and on his tenth visit to the kitchen Farris stopped at the counter and quickly drank several ounces of whiskey. Briefly inspirited, he started a fresh cigarette and took cold beer from the refrigerator. The rest of the whiskey he would save for Sunday, which might be a long day. In his stocking feet he sat on the sofa and watched TV. He sipped some beer, but it did not satisfy and now and then he went to the kitchen for another shot. The hockey out of Buffalo was duller than the game at the Gardens, and so he switched to an old movie starring Lucille Ball and Red Skelton. He thought he remembered seeing it in his hometown with his first wife. And that would have been at least twenty years ago. What happened to the years? How quickly everything goes! And where does it go?

A feeling of immense pity arose within him. Man was a suffering animal whose time on earth was a mere passing moment to, say, the stars. We all live under the same shadow and share the same fate. Emboldened by these serious thoughts, Farris felt somehow united with his fellow creatures in a terrible destiny. When he went to the kitchen for the last time, he returned with the whiskey bottle. And when he poured a measure into his glass, it was with a grave and practiced eye.

It was late when he fell asleep and he once imagined he heard the telephone, though he could have been dreaming. When the apartment buzzer awakened him, he opened his eyes to raw daylight. On the television screen an evangelist in a white suit was preaching to a crowd that hummed and murmured in accord. The apartment buzzer continued to sound and Farris arose, remembering now why he was on the sofa. His child was still missing. Everything must retreat before that awful fact. And it was now past nine o'clock. He switched off the TV and crossed the room to ask in a hoarse whisper who was there. A voice said it was the police. Farris ran a hand through his hair and pressed the button, noting with dismay that this was Sunday and there was only one short drink left in the bottle.

CHAPTER THREE

Before they arrived, he snatched the bottle from the coffee table and took it into the bathroom. There he hurriedly washed his face and swallowed three Anacin tablets. In the mirror he studied his grim looks. Farris detested his worn angular face, though women sometimes found it attractive. Over these past few weeks he had also lost weight, so that now he looked especially haggard. A thin man, nearly six feet tall, with big hands and feet, he was built like his laboring runaway father, if old pictures could be believed. Behind the high forehead and balding temples his dark hair was flecked with gray. He was convinced he looked dissipated.

When he met the detectives at the door, they removed their hats and stepped into his apartment with the blank look of men who had seen such places many times. They were both big and in their thirties, each wearing a light topcoat. One was a Scot, sandy-haired and freckled. He said little. The other man looked younger and had a blond mustache and clear gray eyes.

"Mr. Farris?" he said. "My name is Jack Grahame. I'm a sergeant of detectives with Fifty-one Division. This is my partner, Detective Hamilton."

The big fair-haired man nodded gravely at Farris. Grahame inclined his head and gently massaged his brow as he spoke. "I think we've found your son, Mr. Farris."

Farris's voice wavered. "Where?"

"We'd like you to come along with us, sir, if you would," said Grahame; "we'd like to be sure." Now Farris was certain that something terrible was about to descend upon him, some dreadful summons that would forever change his life. "Is my son dead?" he asked. Looking at their faces, he already knew.

"Yes, I'm afraid he is," said Grahame. "I'm very sorry, sir. We'd like you to come along for a positive ID."

"Identification," the other man said and cleared his throat. Farris felt his legs trembling but he tried hard not to grip the chair. "Why don't you sit down for a minute, sir?" said Grahame. But Farris remained standing. "Where did you find him? What happened to him?"

"We can talk about that on the way down," Grahame said. "Maybe right now you should just sit down for a minute."

"Where do you want me to go?" asked the writer.

Grahame hesitated. "We'd like to take you down to the Coroner's Building. It's not far." And so his young life was over, thought Farris. My son is dead. He is gone forever. How can I deal with this? In his heart he wished himself dead.

"Let me change my shirt," he said. "This shirt looks bad. I slept in it, you see . . . waiting." They nodded. "And I have to shave," said Farris stupidly. "I'll only be a few minutes." He felt somehow like a fool. In the midst of tragedy, the common tasks had to be done.

"Take your time, sir," said Grahame. They were

standing by the window with their hats in their hands.

In the bathroom Farris hastily swallowed what was left in the whiskey bottle and then drank a glass of water. He could hear the detectives talking in low voices, and for a moment he stood by the open bathroom door and tried to understand their words. But even straining to listen, he couldn't make them out. Plugging in his razor, he quickly skimmed his face, pulling the gray skin taut as he rubbed the buzzing machine against his cheeks and under his chin. In his eyes he looked like a man approaching sixty. In the bedroom he pulled on a pair of gray slacks and a forest-green roll-neck sweater, cursing himself for having drunk most of the whiskey the night before. After rinsing his mouth with Listerine, he put on his cord jacket and loafers and went to the front room. "Have you been in touch with the boy's mother?" he asked them. "We don't live together anymore," he added. That fact was obvious; he didn't know why he said it.

"Yes," said Grahame. "We talked to a Mr. Neville. A friend of the family. He's on his way down now."

"He's not a friend of the family," said Farris sullenly, "he's my wife's lover. What's he going for? My son didn't even like him." His remarks remained in the air like a bad odor. The cops looked embarrassed. "Your ex-wife asked him to go, sir," said Grahame.

"I see." And he did.

Pat would now be heavily sedated and unable to cope. Farris had to keep reminding himself that Neville loved her too and was only trying to help. Yet he could not resist feeling indignant at the thought of the young man's being a part of all this. At the door Grahame cleared his throat. "Are you ready to go now, Mr. Farris?" He had lightly gripped Farris's elbow as though the writer were an important but infirm prisoner who must be handled with great care. Farris allowed himself to be helped along like an invalid.

At the elevator they met his neighbor. Dressed in a new fall coat the color of plums, Mrs. Farnsworth was on her way to church. She smiled weakly at the men. "Good morning, Mr. Farris. Have you found your son?"

"Yes. I think so, Mrs. Farnsworth," said Farris. He knew his eyes were damp and he felt humiliated. The men followed the small darting woman into the elevator and they descended in silence. Farris felt his neighbor's eyes upon him. She was far too courteous to ask questions, though, looking at Farris's gaunt, stricken face, it was not difficult to assume the worst. And weren't these two huge men beside him policemen? She hadn't lived in this neighborhood for ten years without being able to recognize policemen when she saw them. And so she now reached out and touched Farris's arm. "If there's anything I can do, Mr. Farris . . ."

"Thank you, Mrs. Farnsworth," said Farris as they stepped into the small lobby with its two plastic armchairs. On the wall was a faded photograph: an aerial view of Toronto in the late fifties. The superintendent had been cleaning the floor and the place stank of disinfectant. A hatless Farris walked between the two detectives as they followed Mrs. Farnsworth into another mild, gray day.

Although it was midmorning, Sherbourne Street looked almost deserted. But the bells of Sacred Heart and St. Luke's were now tolling and a few older people from Fudger House were making their way to service. Across the street a young black woman walked by, clutching a large hymnal to her bosom. The fair-haired cop opened the door of a Plymouth and pushed forward the front seat. As Farris stepped in, he felt oddly criminal. A few of the old folks stared at him as he sat there. They made a U-turn and then headed south. As they passed the brightly clad Mrs. Farnsworth, she smiled again at Farris.

At Carlton they turned westward, with Hamilton tramping the accelerator and moving them easily and quickly through the sparse traffic. In a few minutes they were parked in front of the Coroner's Building on Grenville Street. It was then that Farris leaned forward and asked them who had found his son, and where. Grahame half-turned in his seat to face Farris. "Let's get the ID positive first and then we'll have some coffee and we'll talk. All right, Mr. Farris? The boy we have here has been murdered. Probably suffocation, but we'll have to wait for the coroner's report."

No one spoke as they helped him from the car, and, standing again, Farris breathed in lungfuls of damp, sooty air. Looking across the street he recognized his wife's Mercedes. And Neville was waiting for them inside the entrance, standing next to a security guard. Despite his youthful good looks, his face was gray with fatigue. Keeping Pat calm overnight would not have been easy. Reluctantly Farris shook the young man's hand.

"Let's hope it isn't him, Charlie."

Farris merely nodded as the old security guard talked to the detectives. Then Farris and Neville walked with the detectives to a room where a man in shirt sleeves shook Farris's hand. Farris sensed he was vaguely ill and for a brief moment thought he might pass out. No one spoke as the shirt-sleeved man punched a button on a large closed-circuit television set. A moment later, Farris watched another man from somewhere in the building lift a sheet from Jonathan's face, now pale in death. The dark hair looked crisp. In mercy there were no visible marks; he might have been sleeping. Farris felt Neville touch his arm, but he angrily shook off the touch. "That's him," he whispered, "that's my son."

"Thank you very much, sir," said the man and punched the button. The screen went blank. As they left the room, Neville pressed a handkerchief to his eyes. The shirt-sleeved man sounded apologetic. "If you'd just be good enough to sign a couple of things for us, sir."

"Yes," said Farris. Always there were things to sign. Records had to be maintained. Civilizations depend upon records. He signed.

As he walked away he realized with a pang that the next most important event in his own life would be his own death. How many times had he read of people who had suffered through these ordeals and reported only a feeling of unreality. "I couldn't believe it was happening to me. It was all like a bad dream." But Farris felt nothing like this. In fact, the painful clarity of it struck his eyes like violent sunlight. Everything on this Sunday morning in November was too sharply focused. The cologne from Neville's handkerchief stung his nostrils and the holes in Grahame's heavy pebbled shoes seemed enormous. Farris deeply craved a glass of whiskey.

Standing outside the building, Neville told Farris not to worry about the funeral arrangements. "We'll see to that, Charlie. Don't worry about it." Farris stared at him. It would be hard telling Pat and harder still telling Bill Langford that his grandson had been murdered. This would be a terrible blow for the old man. But it was best that they look after the funeral.

One of Bill's best friends was Tommy Robson of Chambers and Robson. They buried all the old blue-haired dames from Rosedale and quietly looked after the granddaughters who died on abortion tables or in hotel bathrooms. Farris remembered Robson as a regular at Bill's Thursday-night poker games.

"All right," said Farris. "Look, Neville. If Pat. . ." But he didn't finish. What was the point? She didn't need *him* anymore.

"Charlie, I'll phone you as soon as we arrange things. Now that we know, we want it over as quickly as possible, don't we?" Farris looked down the empty street. It was Sunday morning and he was standing outside the Coroner's Building talking to *his* wife's lover about funeral arrangements for *his* son. How bizarre could your life get? Peter Neville was talking about newspaper and TV people, the media, as he called them. "Once they get hold of this, Charlie, they'll hound you and Pat to death. The murder of a child! It's rather sensational. We've got to get the funeral over with quickly. We've got to maintain some dignity here." Neville was frowning. Perhaps he already saw himself protecting Pat by shoving aside newspaper photographers. But this talk of dignity! It was one of those words Farris had never understood. Where was the dignity in drinking beer and watching TV football while your son was being murdered? And maybe that was why this man was now in his wife's bed.

"Let me know what you arrange," said Farris.

"All right, Charlie. Take care of yourself."

The two detectives had stood apart, and now Neville walked over and spoke briefly to them. Farris looked across the street where they sold imported rugs. He watched Neville walk across to the Mercedes, a tall, slim, boyish figure. The young man jogged every day. For a while Pat ran with him, though Farris knew that wouldn't last because she grew too easily bored with exercise. Nevertheless, during cold evenings last spring Farris had sat in his car behind a newspaper and watched the two of them come out of her building in matching blue running suits. They jogged westward toward Bedford Road, and if they saw him they took no notice. And watching them, he felt ridiculous, a comic figure, filled with self-loathing. Yet he had returned on other evenings.

Now the two detectives walked over to him, and again Farris asked them about his son and where he had been found. "Let's get away from here," said Grahame. "We can talk in the car." The Mercedes pulled away swiftly and Neville waved as he passed. Nobody returned the wave. In the Plymouth, Grahame sat in the backseat with Farris. They both smoked from Grahame's package. "I'm sorry, Mr. Farris. This is tough. But maybe the worst is over. Now you've seen him and you know." They smoked for a moment in silence and then Grahame spoke again. "He was found about three hours ago down on the Esplanade, east of Sherbourne. Behind a factory, in some long grass. Would you like some coffee? There's a McDonald's right up at the corner."

"No coffee," said Farris.

"Well, that's okay." Grahame touched his partner on the shoulder. "I think we better take Mr. Farris home now, Doug. We can talk along the way."

"All right," said Hamilton and started the car. Grahame inhaled deeply. "He was wrapped in two garbage bags. The guys who found him noticed the shape of a body inside these bags, so they flagged down a patrol car. Then we were called."

"Who were they? Who found him?" Farris was appalled. His son's life had ended in garbage bags at the back of a factory! Who would do such a thing to him? He felt the hatred burning like acid along his veins.

"A couple of winos found him. They'd gone behind the factory looking for bottles."

"What about them? Could they have done it?"

The traffic along Carlton Street was thickening. In front of Maple Leaf Gardens a group of elderly sightseers from the Carlton Inn were climbing aboard a bus. Grahame seemed to be arranging his answer. "No, we don't think they had anything to do with it. We've checked them out, Mr. Farris. They ate their dinner and spent the whole night at the Sally Ann. Lots of people saw them. We'll have to wait for the coroner's report, but I'd say your son had been dead for several hours before they found him. And then, if they had anything to do with it, I don't think they'd hail a patrol car. No, these guys just found the body and, believe me, they were very upset when they found it was a child. One guy was in tears." Listening, Farris looked out the window at all the fortunate people with their small, everyday miseries.

"Don't worry, sir," said Grahame. "We'll get the person or persons responsible for this. Every policeman in the city will be looking for him." Farris could only blink tears and no one said anything more until they pulled up in front of his apartment building. Grahame got out with him and they stood on the sidewalk.

"Go in and have yourself a good stiff drink, Mr. Farris. We'll be back in touch with you. But I just want to be sure we've got it straight before we go. Now, according to your statement to Constable Huckle, your son left your apartment about three. Right?" Farris nodded.

"You're sure about the time, give or take five minutes? All right? Now, he was on his way to the store for candy. That's the store around that corner down there on Carlton Street. The northwest corner. Right?" He pointed southward as he spoke.

"Yes," said Farris.

"And this was not unusual? He did this every time he spent a Saturday afternoon with you. And usually he'd be gone how long? Twenty minutes? Half an hour?"

"Never more than half an hour," said Farris. "I've told you people all this before."

"Right. And I won't bother you anymore at this time. But listen, just one more question which might be important. Did Jonathan ever mention meeting anyone during his trip to the store? You know, did he ever come in and say, 'Well, I saw so and so again today and we talked for a minute.' You know, maybe a person his own age or an adult who had seemed friendly toward him."

"No, nothing like that," said Farris, "he never mentioned meeting anybody."

Grahame flicked his cigarette onto the road. "Well, think about it anyway because it might be important. Anything, however small, that he might have said could be useful."

"I'll think about it," said Farris.

"That's fine. That's all we can ask. If he didn't say anything, he didn't say anything. But sometimes, you know, when you really concentrate, you can remember some little thing he might have mentioned about a particular person. And it could be helpful." He moved around the car, and then Farris asked, "Was my son sexually molested, Sergeant?"

Grahame massaged his brow. "I wouldn't like to say at this moment, Mr. Farris. We'll just have to wait for the pathologist's report on that. We'll know by this afternoon."

"But it usually happens in these cases, doesn't it?" insisted Farris.

"Yes, it does . . . usually," said Grahame. "Goodbye, Mr. Farris." He got into the car as Farris turned toward his building.

And at his apartment door a surprise! Leaning against the door was a paper bag. And inside the bag was a bottle of Gordon's gin and a message from his neighbor on blue scented paper.

> Mister Farris
> I think you must be going through some dreadful ordeal at the moment. Perhaps you can use this to steady your nerves.
>
> Kindest regards,
> Marjorie Farnsworth

Entering his apartment, he clutched the bag against his chest, cherishing this gift from a fellow drunk who knew the liquor stores were closed on Sundays. He resisted the impulse to thank her. Instead he mixed some gin with Tang. After three stiff drinks, he felt calm enough to sit down and wonder with bitterness what to do with the rest of his life.

CHAPTER FOUR

Lying on the couch, he fell asleep and dreamed of walking with his wife on a country road in England. Then the telephone was ringing and his son's murder was with him again like a long shadow across his life. When he answered the phone, it was Peter Neville. "I've told them, Charlie," he said. "Pat is now under the doctor's orders. She's taken a mild sedative and is lying down. Father Buckley is with her. She's being very brave, actually. How are you?"

"I'm alive," said Farris coldly. Neville ignored the hostility in Farris's voice. "Poor Bill. I just came from telling *him*. He sits alone and weeps. I couldn't persuade him to come here and stay with Pat for a few days." Probably because he doesn't like you, thought Farris. That damn fancy-pants Englishman she's now going with. That's how Bill once described Neville to Farris.

"He asked about you, Charlie. He said, 'Give my love to Charlie.' " Yes. He would say something like that, thought Farris. Sentimental old Bill. He and Farris had always gotten along and the writer had always considered his father-in-law to be a singularly fortunate man. For over sixty years his life was unblemished by misfortune. He and his wife were both rich. There were two healthy, loving children who gave them no major problems, except briefly in the sixties when Teddy took to wearing beads and playing the guitar and smoking cannabis. But he soon got over that, and now developed suburban shopping centers and made a great deal of money. And then, after sixty-six years of happiness and success, Bill Langford's life had come apart at the seams. Within the past two years he had lost his wife to cancer, watched his ancient mother decline into senility, witnessed the ruin of his daughter's marriage and the imminent ruin of his son's. Now his beloved grandson was dead. Farris liked the man and felt sorry for him. Neville was talking about the funeral arrangements. "I phoned Tom Robson and he's arranged for the funeral tomorrow afternoon at St. James. Two o'clock. There will be a short service at the cemetery chapel and interment in the Langford plot. Later in the week Father Buckley will arrange a private mass for the family. Is all this agreeable to you, Charlie?"

"Yes," said Farris dully. Would it make any difference if it wasn't? Neville cleared his throat. "I understand the media have already got hold of this. Someone said he heard it on the two o'clock radio news. We've got to be sure that Jonathan's funeral doesn't turn into some sort of media circus." He paused. "Charlie?"

"Yes," said Farris. He seemed to have relinquished control of an important part of his life. Neville had taken over the running of his family during a critical time and Farris felt vaguely reduced.

"Just a minute, Charlie. Father Buckley wants a word with you." Farris braced himself. He had never liked Bunny Buckley and, behind the hearty cordiality, the priest didn't like him either. To Farris, Buckley was more like a high school football coach with his large, florid face and his sports stories. But he was well liked and Farris remembered Bill Langford once saying that if Bunny had had more ambition, he might have been a bishop. An old friend of the Langford's, Buckley had married Farris and Pat thirteen years ago. A year later he had christened Jonathan. Now Farris heard the rich, firm voice. "Charles, I'm praying for you. This is a terrible tragedy." Farris said nothing. It was *his* son who was dead. What did Buckley know? Farris refused to help him with words, and he thought he could hear the priest breathing heavily through the stiff hairs in his nose. "If there's anything at all I can do, Charles." If he mentions God and his mysterious ways, thought Farris, I'll hang up in his ear. But he knew that Buckley was too clever for that.

"Charles, I don't know if Peter mentioned tonight to you. The family is gathering at Tommy Robson's at eight o'clock. Jonathan will be there. This is just for the family, Charles. Patricia wants the funeral tomorrow. I suggested Tuesday with a requiem mass, but she said not. We'll have a mass later in the week when things quieten down. The main thing now is to give the child a decent burial. I'll see you tonight, Charles. Please believe that I am praying for both you and Patricia."

"Yes. Right."

"I'll see you this evening, Charles. Good-bye."

"Good-bye."

Farris made himself a sandwich and boiled water

for tea, noting how his large hands shook as he took down the cup and saucer from the cupboard. The hot tea burned his throat and he was glad. He wondered how Jonathan felt just before he died. The terror of it! Grahame mentioned suffocation. Thinking about his child's dying moments left Farris utterly abject. The knock on the door startled him. He wasn't expecting anyone, nor did he wish particularly to speak to anyone. Then he thought it must be his neighbor, who by now would have heard the news. But when he opened the door he saw Tony Murchison, a columnist with one of the morning newspapers.

The sallow-faced Murchison plucked off a tweed cap and stuck out a hand. "Charlie. I'm sorry, believe me." The columnist looked sick, but then he had always looked like that. Farris had worked a few desks away from him a dozen years ago when Murchison covered City Hall. Now he wrote a column that newspaper people called human interest. Farris didn't like the column or the columnist and years ago there had been an incident at a party. Murchison had whispered something lewd to Pat and he might even have touched her. Farris was drunk at the time and unclear about details. But there was some pushing and Farris landed a glancing blow against Murchison's cheek. Friends had parted them. Now the man stood in Farris's living room. "May I sit down, Charlie?"

Farris waved him to a chair, wondering how the man had got in the building. He must have followed someone through the lobby door. "Do you have any cigarettes, Murchison?" Farris asked.

The man looked relieved to be asked such an innocent question. "I don't, Charlie. I'm sorry. I gave them up several years ago. But look, I can phone for some." He was on his feet. "It'll just take a minute. What kind do you smoke? I'll order a carton."

"Forget it," said Farris.

"No really, I mean it, Charlie. It's as easy as picking up a phone. I'll get you cigarettes."

"Fuck it, Murchison," Farris said angrily. "Just leave it, all right? Forget the fucking cigarettes. What do you want anyway?" It felt suddenly good to be irritable like this, and, looking at Murchison's thin jaw, he wished now that he had managed a sharper, cleaner blow at that party. He might have taken him right out with a better punch and that would have been more satisfying than all that back-slapping and phony accord that friends had wished upon them afterward. He thought he could now remember shaking hands after the fight, and the memory was loathsome to him.

"Listen," said Murchison. "About that party. No hard feelings, Charlie. When you hit me. Remember?" Farris plunged his hands into his pockets and looked at the man. Murchison leaned forward. "Charlie, I've just heard about your personal tragedy. It's terrible. We've got to get the son of a bitch who did this."

"What are you after, Murchison?"

"Charlie, I want to help you and I can. I have thousands of readers. Tell me what happened yesterday. I want to help."

"Like hell you do, you want a story."

"That too, of course. I'm a professional newspaperman."

Farris looked away and cursed under his breath. He felt like a drink, but didn't want to touch the stuff in front of Murchison. The columnist looked over at him. "Listen, Charlie, I know what you're going through." Farris glared at him so fiercely that he looked away. "All right, that was a fatuous remark. I'm sorry. But at least I can imagine what you're going through. But listen, when the media get hold of this, it's going to be big news. Child murders are headlines. People are definitely interested. I'd like to get *your* story. I could do it with some taste." Farris looked down at the man. "You never did anything with taste in your fucking simple-minded life, Murchison." Murchison twirled his tweed cap on a forefinger. "The TV people are merciless, Charlie. They'll bug your ass off at a time when you want peace and quiet. They'll push a microphone in your face as you walk out your door. I hate those bastards." His voice had risen.

"I'm not telling you anything, Murchison," said Farris.

The columnist gave him a sour look. "Are you divorced now, Charlie, or just separated? I remember your wife, a lovely woman." Farris said nothing. Murchison had now stood up and was adjusting his absurd cap. "You'd better get used to being news, Charlie, because you're going to be news over the next few days." He sounded bitter. "I'm trying to help you. If you give me your side of things you won't be bugged so much by the others. You're an old newspaperman yourself, Charlie, you know that." He was standing by the door in his Burberry and tweed cap. He now looked annoyed. Farris had sat down and leaned his head back. He felt weary and empty. Closing his eyes, he tried to imagine how he felt two days ago before all this. "Are you working these days, Charlie?" asked Murchison. "I haven't seen anything from you in months."

"Fuck you, Murchison," said Farris hoarsely, his

eyes still closed. At the door Murchison said, "I'm just doing my job, Farris. I *am* sorry about your son." As he left he softly closed the door behind him.

CHAPTER FIVE

Tremulous yet sober, Farris climbed the subway stairs at St. Clair Station and walked eastward a few blocks. The night air was cool and damp. Winter was out there waiting, but this long, mild fall was not yet prepared to yield. In front of the funeral home a solitary light burned across the doorway, and a family of strangers moved past the iron gate and up the stone steps. Standing there, Farris wondered briefly if he had misunderstood Buckley. Perhaps he had said tomorrow night. But when he opened the heavy front door he immediately saw Tommy Robson, who nodded to him and came forward. The other grieving family was now being shepherded into a room off the hallway. Farris sniffed the warm, odorous air and remembered his mother's face in a coffin years ago. Robson, a small rosy-colored man in mourning suit and waistcoat, offered a hand in greeting. "Charlie. I'm so sorry about all this. Let me take your coat. If you'll come this way." He turned and escorted Farris down the hallway to a large room.

The light in the room was subdued except at the far end where the open coffin lay. There it seemed harsh and violent as it spilled over the rich dark wood and ruffled satin. Farris turned his eyes away from the glare. In the room were several people he didn't know. Most likely they were cousins and uncles and aunts. Beside him, Robson asked if he might be excused and quietly departed. On the other side of the room Pat was seated on a sofa. Her sister-in-law, Sylvia, was holding her hand, and to Farris this was strange, for the two women really didn't like each other. Nearby stood Bill Langford, pale and somehow shrunken in one of his large tentlike suits. He seemed to have aged twenty years since Farris last saw him only months ago. And beside him were Teddy and Father Buckley and Peter Neville and a tall slender woman Farris didn't recognize.

When Pat saw him, she rose and crossed the room. People parted to let her pass, and they watched her with sadness and concern in their eyes. She had been weeping heavily and her face shone as though scrubbed. The murmuring ceased as people watched. Pat held forth her two hands and Farris seized them. They were clammy and her nails bit into his flesh as they stood without embracing. And with horror, Farris realized that they were to be spared nothing; they could no longer even comfort one another. Their child was dead and so was their life together. Pat's voice was barely a whisper. "He's gone, Charlie. Our boy has gone." Farris brushed his lips against her knuckles, willing himself not to weep.

And then Bill Langford came across the room and put his arms around them and hugged them. His voice was harsh and cracked. "My God, kids . . . I pray with all my heart that you'll both get through this." He hugged Farris tightly. "Charlie, I've missed you. Why didn't you come around to see me?" Farris stared at the swollen eyes and kindly face now stupid with grief. "I'm sorry, Bill." He looked toward the

coffin. "I want to see him now." And he walked to
the far end of the room, aware that others were
watching him. Standing there, he looked down at the
pale, stern face. Jonathan was still frowning. It was
one of Farris's major regrets that his son hadn't
laughed more in life. He seemed to have taken the
whole question of existence so seriously. Even as a
little boy, he had preferred to play by himself for
hours, sorting out games and toys with a puzzled
scowl on his face. Farris often used to wish it were
otherwise. Now he was gone. Finished. This was it,
and the writer was struck by the simplicity of death.
In many ways it was immensely appealing and the
idea moved him. Then he turned and walked away,
standing back against a wall. He looked around for
Grandmother Langford, but she seemed to be the
only one not here. He missed that tough old woman
with her harsh, unsentimental view of things. Her
tongue had terrorized the family for over eighty
years. But now she was mostly beyond things, and it
was probably just as well that she wasn't around.
Still, she hadn't missed a family gathering in her life
and would be furious when she discovered the truth.
Holed up in that nursing home, she still subscribed to
Scientific American and *The Atlantic Monthly*. Last
year, a week before Christmas, the Langfords had
thrown a four-generation party on the old woman's
eighty-seventh birthday. On that occasion she had
cornered Farris with questions about his writing. She
was the only member of the family who considered
writing a serious occupation. As a young girl she had
written romantic novels that were never published,
and she once ran away to New York and had a leg-
endary affair with a famous American poet. Or so the
story went.

Then, at the party, she had pointed to Jonathan standing with his young twin cousins. At that moment, Jonathan chose to look over at his father and make a face expressing extreme boredom. And Lavinia Langford asked Farris, "Charlie, who is that boy? Is he a Langford? He rather looks like us."

"Yes," said Farris. "That's Jonathan. He's your great-grandson." The old woman's mind cleared briefly and she frowned. "Well, what in heaven's name is he making that absurd face for? Is he not well?"

And she was once one of Toronto's great society beauties. She had entertained royalty; her dinner parties were famous. Now her urine was collected in a rubber bottle strapped to her leg. And so the four of them had posed for the photographer that afternoon, the oldest peevish and forgetful, the youngest fidgety and bored. Throughout, Pat smiled but seemed abstracted, distanced from it all. Later she hurried away to her lover. And Farris now believed that that occasion was bad luck—a family's boast that it could flourish through four generations.

Teddy and Sylvia Langford came across the room to see him. Now thirty, Teddy was built like his father, bearlike, with heavy shoulders and a big shaggy head of coarse dark hair. He looked like an aging linebacker gone to seed, and in fact had played college football before joining the flower crowd. Now he looked seriously overweight and his color was unhealthy. Although he belonged to several clubs, he claimed that business kept him too busy to work out. Despite the weight and the bad color, his baby face looked much as it did ten years ago when he worried his father by wearing beads and carrying placards in anti-Vietnam demonstrations. Many nights Farris had killed a bottle of scotch with Bill Langford, assuring his father-in-law that Teddy would soon redeem himself. It was in his blood to make money. Now he was in real estate and rich. However, his marriage was not working and there was talk of a separation. Last summer Sylvia took their six-year-old twin daughters and visited her parents in Calgary for several weeks. Nobody seemed to miss anybody during that time. Like his father, Teddy was a toucher, and now embraced Farris and uttered his name in a voice choked with emotion. Sylvia, thin and blond, kissed Farris lightly on the cheek. Farris tried to look beyond them to see his wife, but she was hidden from his view by people.

Teddy gripped Farris's shoulder. "Charlie? Do the cops have anything going on this?" Farris felt suddenly weary and depleted by the question. Yes. There was all that to go through yet. Someone was responsible for all this. But now was not the time. Now they must mourn the loss of his son's young life. He sounded tired. "I couldn't say, Teddy. I haven't spoken to them since this morning." "What kind of dirty son of a bitch would do that to a kid?" Teddy proffered the question in the tone of a man mystified by all forms of universal injustice. But his wife made a small wry face. "Teddy? This is not the place for that kind of talk. All right?" Sylvia's voice was high-pitched and clamorous; she was a born scold. Nevertheless, she was right. Beneath the heavy platinum hair her face was stormy, and Farris guessed they'd be quarreling all evening. Teddy loosened his tie and leaned in on Farris. "This goddamn city is getting as bad as New York or Chicago." Sylvia plucked at his sleeve like a child. "Save that stuff for later, will you, please?" But Teddy ignored her and addressed Farris, hungry for information. "Charlie? I'm asking you straight out. Was Johnny molested? Was this a sexual crime?"

"Jesus Christ," said Sylvia, turning away from them.

"I don't know, Teddy," said Farris. "I haven't heard yet."

"Well, what did the coroner say?" Teddy inherited this ruthless candor from his mother, who would never beat around the bush if she could club something head-on. Farris well remembered her favorite question to him: "Well, Charles, are you working now or just writing?" But at the moment Teddy was being a pain in the ass and Farris sounded impatient with him.

"I haven't been in touch with the coroner, Ted. There'll be time enough for that. Right now is not the time."

"Yes, Ted," said Sylvia sarcastically. "As Charlie says, this is not the time or the place. So please don't make a fool of yourself." Teddy turned to her and whispered, "Who is making a fool of himself, for fuck sakes? You watch your mouth, Syl, or I'll belt you later. I already owe you."

"Oh sure," said Sylvia, but her eyes looked frightened. Teddy now whispered like a conspirator. "Charlie, the son of a bitch who did this has got to be caught. And when he is, he should be strung up by the balls right on the City Hall steps. This goddamn city has got so many weirdos in it anymore. That's right, little wife, you go right on looking at me that way, but I know what I'm talking about. By the balls. That's how I'd hang him and right . . . on . . . the . . . City . . . Hall . . . steps." He punctuated his last few words with a thick forefinger on Sylvia's shoulder.

She smiled at Farris. "I'm going over to see Pat now. Take it easy, Charlie."

Farris nodded and watched her walk away, a slim, fine-looking woman who somehow couldn't put it together. He felt sorry for her and hoped she would get out on her own. She was an outsider who had never been accepted by the Langford clan. Nobody had approved of the marriage and Teddy's mother had openly disliked her daughter-in-law. Even Bill with his great good nature could not bring himself to say many kind things about her. He was convinced she was frigid and that was why Teddy ran around. Thus Sylvia was tolerated only because she was Teddy's wife and the mother of his daughters.

Again Teddy leaned in on Farris and whispered. "Do you want some coke? I've got a few crystals." He patted his suit pocket.

"No thanks, Ted. I don't use it. I'm a soaker from way back."

"This is good stuff, Charlie. It'll clear your head. No one will know. We can go in the washroom."

"No, it's all right, Ted, forget it."

"Okay," said Teddy, "but if you need anything at all, old buddy, you just let me know." Farris liked his brother-in-law least when he affected this old fraternity-house amiability.

"We're going to put up some money for this, Charlie," said Teddy.

Farris looked at him. "What?"

"My company. Me and my partners. I talked to Benny and Phil on the phone about it this afternoon. They've got great respect for our family. They hate this kind of dirt. Phil says this could happen to anyone. He's got two sons, twelve and ten. We'd like to put up twenty big ones to start. But that's just a beginning. Phil thinks there's some kind of tax thing that can be worked out, but that's not what matters really. What matters is catching the son of a bitch."

Bill Langford was now standing alongside them, stroking his long, sad face. Teddy put an arm around his father's shoulders. "Dad, I was just telling Charlie. We're going to put up some reward money. The company, that is. We're going to get this son of a bitch. We figure we'll start at twenty thousand and see what happens. But there has to be an arrest and conviction or no deal."

"Ted?" said Farris. "Why don't you just leave it for now? Just shut up about it."

The big man looked puzzled and hurt. "Well, sure, Charlie. But look, I'm just trying to be helpful."

"All right, Teddy, we know that," said his father, "but we'll talk about all that later."

"Sure, Dad. That's fine by me."

The three men stood in clumsy silence listening to other voices, then Farris asked about Grandmother Langford. As Bill spoke, Farris smelled the whiskey on his father-in-law's breath. "About the same, Charlie. We haven't told her about this yet, but I'm going to have to. I don't want her to hear this from somebody else. She keeps up with everything, you know, reads the papers, watches the television news. She'll forget what she sees five minutes later, but she still sees it. And for those five minutes she can be damned accurate, let me tell you. I've phoned the Manor and told them to keep her away from the television room at eleven o'clock. And one of the nurses took the radio out of her room. She said it needed repairs. But I'm going to have to tell her tomorrow morning. We can't keep her from watching television or reading her *Globe*. She'll insist on coming along to the funeral and I don't see how we can very well refuse her." Bill's eyes were filling with tears. "It's just too goddamn bad that an old woman like that couldn't be spared this kind of thing near the end of her life." Farris thought that Bill might just as well be speaking for himself, and perhaps he was. He was now shaking out an immense white handkerchief and pressing it against his eyes. "I'm sorry, Charlie, but goddamn it to hell, this is the finish of me. I've never seen anything to beat this. It's terrible. This is the goddamnest . . . God, the boy was everything to me."

As his father-in-law held the handkerchief to his face, Farris felt riven by pity and rage. That they should all suffer like this. That his son's portion in life should be so small. It was all so unforgivably wrong. "We've got to get through this, Bill. These next few days."

"I loved that boy, Charlie." His words sounded strangled. "I don't think anyone could love a person the way I loved him. And now he's gone. Why? That's what I'd like to know. Why?" "Take it easy, Daddy, please," said Teddy helplessly. Pat had hurried across the room to be with her father. "Okay, Dad," she said. "Let's take a seat now. Let's just sit down over here nice and easy. Bunny's here now." And the Anglican priest, his big silver head wagging gravely, took his friend's arm and led him to a chair. "Come on now, Willy. Let's sit down for a few minutes."

Overcome, Teddy watched his father. "You mark my words, Charlie. We're going to get whoever did this. If the money won't do it, I've got friends. They'll break kneecaps if they have to. They hate this kind of stuff."

Teddy occasionally bragged of his Mafia connections. Farris doubted whether his brother-in-law was a serious gangster groupie. Still, you never knew. He was terrifically sentimental about the mob. According to him, they were all fine family men who paid their taxes and took their children to ball games. But Pat was having none of this stuff about broken kneecaps. "For God sakes, Teddy, stop that kind of talk. Don't get mixed up in anything you can't handle. And don't bring in any of your thug friends. I won't have it. Let the police look after this."

"The cops in this town are out to lunch, Patty."

"The cops in this town are *not* out to lunch, as you put it. Now just leave it alone."

"Christ!" Teddy looked bewildered. "I just want to help. . . This is all too much. . ." Pat leaned forward and kissed him on the cheek. "I know. . . I know. . ." They held each other tightly. "Look, I want to talk to Charlie now," said Pat. "Okay?"

"Sure, Patty. But I'm here when you need me. All right?"

"I know that."

Teddy walked over to his father, who was listening to Buckley and pressing the white cloth against his face. Farris felt overpowered by them all. The Langfords had a way of smothering you and excluding you all at the same time. He had seen his dead son. Now, more than anything, he wanted this to be over and he devoutly wished the funeral were this evening. "I need a cigarette," he said, "Let's get out of here." She took his arm and her touch sent a shock through him. In the corner, Peter Neville watched them leave the room like man and wife. And for the time it takes to cross a room, Farris felt exalted and whole.

In the hallway, strangers headed for other rooms to mourn and by a small lectern an old man stooped to sign a guest book. In a kind of vestibule off the main entrance, Farris smoked by a small window bearing a

Celtic cross. After a moment Pat said quietly, "I dread tomorrow." Farris said nothing. "It will be splashed across every newspaper and television screen in Ontario. I'm sure they'll be at the cemetery. For God sakes, Charlie, don't attack anyone tomorrow. I know that temper of yours. But remember, that's just what the bastards would like. An incident that would turn it into a circus. Peter may be of some help here. He's talked to some of his friends at the CBC and they'll do the best they can. But it is news, and when some of these people see a story, they just don't know when to stop."

An angry and brooding Farris looked out at the street. "Fuck them. Who cares about that? Our son is dead. What do I care what they think or do? But if one of them shoves a microphone in my face tomorrow, I'm liable to ram it down his throat."

"And that's just exactly what I don't want." She looked at him sadly. "Charlie. Please. Tomorrow don't drink. Take a couple of Valium, but don't drink."

"You Langfords are in a drug-dispensing mood this evening. Earlier your brother offered me some cocaine."

"I'm just asking you, Charlie. Please. I want Jonathan's funeral to have some dignity."

There was that word again, and Farris slammed the end of his fist against the wall. The panes in the little window shuddered. "Dignity! That's all I've been hearing today. Well, let me tell you something, Pat. There is no fucking dignity in the kind of death Johnny suffered last night. He died cruelly and violently, and if I think too much about it, I know I'll lose my mind. But tomorrow we bury him. The worst thing that could possibly happen to me has happened. And tomorrow I will see my son put into the ground. . ." His voice cracked and Pat touched his arm.

"Charlie . . . please."

But he was crying and his voice was thick.

"You talk about dignity, but I have to say this, Pat. I'm never going to see his face again and so . . ." He grasped her wrist. "It's a day for lamentation . . . lamentations, Pat. I may come on like a Mediterranean peasant and throw myself in the grave. I may rend my garments and wail. . . I don't know." His voice was barely a hoarse whisper. "But I know I'm not going to be too fucking worried about what people in this town or any town think." He released her wrist and stabbed an ashtray with his cigarette. "And drink? You better believe I'm going to have a drink. I'm going to have ten fucking drinks. And maybe ten more after that. I don't intend to sober up for a long time."

There were tears in Pat's eyes. "Charlie? For Jon's sake . . ."

"No, Pat. It's for your sake. And the holy Langford family."

Pat stood in the corner with her clenched fists to her face. Then she placed the thumbs under her chin. Farris remembered her doing this when she was peculiarly anxious about something. It made her look so young and vulnerable. She shook her head. "I just don't know if I can take that graveside bit." She seemed to be talking aloud to herself. Nothing more was said for what seemed a long time. They were briefly sealed in their own memories of the child they once shared. Farris had lighted another cigarette and now looked through the doorway at the people leaving. A man his own age walked beside an elderly woman who clung to his arm for support. Were they burying a husband and father tomorrow? Farris guessed it likely. It was now past nine o'clock. It would be a long night, and he doubted whether there would be much sleep in it for him. He tried to remember how much gin was left. Then Pat said, "I'm going away after the funeral. Just for a couple of weeks. I talked to Dr. Toomey. He phoned from Philadelphia and he thinks it might be a good idea to get away for a while. Not long, maybe ten days or a couple of weeks."

Farris wiped his eyes with a handkerchief. "Where are you going?" he asked, watching the man help his mother with her coat.

"I'm not sure yet. It doesn't really matter as long as it isn't somewhere that has associations. So that rules out the cottage or Florida. But Peter is looking after it. Perhaps the Cayman Islands."

Farris looked across at her. "Where the hell is that?"

"In the West Indies."

"Is he going with you?"

"Who? Peter?"

"Yes," said Farris dryly, "Peter."

"Of course. He's been a tremendous help to me, Charlie. I couldn't have gone through this without him." Farris looked away again and Pat continued, "Charlie . . . I'm in love with him. Can't you understand that? I have been now for a couple of years. We're going to be married one day."

"Is he good in bed?"

She sighed. "You would ask that, wouldn't you? All right, yes he is. But that's not the most important thing. He's kind and considerate and listens to me. He's good to be with. He's good to me. He's good *for* me."

"He's also ten years younger than you," said Farris. "It's ridiculous."

"I don't want to talk about this anymore, Charlie. It's pointless."

"All right then, let's not talk about it." He sounded like a sulky child and he hated himself for sounding this way. Yet he was deeply hurt by the thought that she would soon be far away from all this. It seemed somehow like a betrayal. "Don't you care if they catch the bastard who did this?" he asked. It seemed such an illogical question that Pat frowned. "Of course I care. What's more, I have every confidence in the police. I've talked to them and they've assured me that they will find him. They said it may very well turn out to be the biggest manhunt in the city's history. They'll get him, Charlie. But my being here isn't going to do anything about that. I just have to get away from this atmosphere. . ."

"You do what you think best," said Farris nastily.

Pat flushed. "Oh, for God sakes, Charlie. Do you think I'm going to be down on some tropical beach, lying in the sun, drinking rum Collins and not caring about anything? What kind of mother do you think I am? That's my only child in there, goddamn it. I'll never have another one."

"Neither will I, by Christ," he said savagely. But she was right. There was no good reason for her to stay in this town. "I'm sorry," he muttered.

Pat said nothing for a moment and then asked, "What about you? What do you think you'll do?"

"I'm staying," said Farris in a flat voice.

"Well . . . you'd better change your phone number and give the new listing only to the police and close friends. That's what they told me. If you don't, you'll be plagued with crank calls."

"I'll think about it." He still felt resentful and abandoned. "All right, Charlie," said Pat, leaning forward and kissing him on the cheek. It was worse than not touching; it was like the blessing of an indulgent aunt. "I'll see you tomorrow. We'll pick you up about a quarter to two."

"Fine." He watched her walk away. Perhaps it was the drugs that steadied her.

But when Farris left the funeral home, he was seething. In the mellow late-autumn night he walked the streets to calm himself. Overhead the moon, a great round thing, rolled through light clouds, plunging the sides of buildings and houses into darkness and then swiftly lighting the path before him. When his son was small, Farris had taken him out one night to see the man in the moon, pointing out the eyes and nose and mouth while the child clung to his neck and looked up with serious eyes at the heavens. Now, embittered by the memory, Farris walked the city streets, sometimes forgetting himself and losing his way. It took him two bitter hours to reach the Del Monte Arms.

CHAPTER SIX

After a few hours of exhausted sleep Farris again awakened to his son's death. Now he would have to live with it each waking day. And today they would put Jonathan in the ground alongside Langfords who had lain there for a hundred and fifty years. Farris and Pat and the boy had walked by the old family plot one leafy summer morning years ago; Johnny would have been six. He was filled with questions. Who was under the ground there? What did he look like now? Was he just bones? Did he have hair? A boy at school said that dead people's fingernails and hair grew, and that under the ground were millions of skeletons with long hair and fingernails. Pat showed him the graves of his forebears. There was his great-grandfather Langford, Grandpa's father and Grandma Vinny's husband. And there was a cousin who had drowned in Georgian Bay within sight of the family cottage. And that's why you have to be careful when you go swimming. And who is that over there under the gray stone with the angel? That was your Grandpa's younger brother Richard. They called him Dick. Dead at the age of six in 1921. The boy was interested in this and questioned his mother closely. But that's my age. How did he die? Jonathan sounded outraged and Pat took his hand. Uncle Dick died of a disease called meningitis. Will I die of that? No, of course not, darling. Boys and girls don't die of that nowadays. We have medicine for that now. And Jonathan had said nothing more, but looked thoughtful as they walked among the trees and gravestones. On the other side of the black iron fence the traffic blared. Later they ate ice cream and went to a Disney film. It was a bad day to remember such things.

In the shower he let the hot needles of water punish his body. At one time not so long ago he had been in good shape; now he was less so. To Farris his gray flesh looked slack and faintly repulsive. Yet he couldn't bring himself to run in the streets like other men. After dressing hurriedly and drinking a cup of tea, he went out to buy whiskey and a bottle of gin for Mrs. Farnsworth. He promised himself to be careful, but he knew he'd need several drinks before the funeral.

When he returned, he laid out the *Globe* on the coffee table and read about the murder. The front page carried Jonathan's school picture. According to the paper, no suspects had yet been arrested. Inside was Tony Murchison's column, entitled "Visit to a Grief-Stricken Dad." It was an absurdly sentimental piece in which Murchison made it appear as though he and Farris were old friends. Farris read it slowly with disgust. At eleven o'clock he opened a bottle of Teacher's and had his first drink of the day. The first one was always the best, with your mind not yet clouded over and the whiskey doing its job. You still had the illusion of control. And this is how things were with Farris. He was coping, and in an obscure way he felt proud of himself. In a little while the worst would be over. He drank slowly and carefully, pacing himself, for there were boundaries he was determined not to cross during the next few hours. He would seek a level beyond pain but inside propriety. When Pat phoned, he was feeling about right, all things considered.

"How are you today, Charlie?"

"I'm all right. Everything's fine. I'm ready."

"Are you sure you're okay?"

"Listen, Pat, if you're trying to find out whether I'm drunk or not, forget it. I'm fine."

"All right, Charlie, I believe you. We'll pick you up at a quarter to two."

"I can walk. It's not far."

"I don't think that's wise. One of Robson's men has been over to the cemetery this morning. One of the stations is setting up TV cameras. Now, you'll avoid a big hassle if you just get in the car when it arrives." Farris sipped his scotch. What she said made sense.

"All right."

"Fine. I'll see you at a quarter to two." She paused. "Incidentally, the police think they've found the man who did it."

Farris's heart leaped. "What?"

"They think it's the man."

"When were you talking to them?"

"An hour ago. They haven't released a name. This man has a long record as a sex criminal, and in fact he's only been out of prison a few weeks."

"Do they know for certain this is the guy? Has he confessed? Have they charged him?"

"No, I don't think so," she said, "but they're gathering evidence. He doesn't seem to be able to account for his whereabouts on Saturday night. And he lives in that area. So . . ."

Farris merely grunted. He'd phone the cops himself.

"We'll pick you up at a quarter to two, Charlie. In front of your apartment building."

"Yes. I'll see you then."

He hung up and then dialed the cops' number. Grahame was out, and though the man at the desk was friendly enough, he wasn't giving anything away. Yes, they had a suspect, but as for his name, forget it; it was much too early for names. Farris hung up feeling dispirited. He wanted to put a name on the killer; it seemed suddenly very important to him. The guy must have a name. Was it John, Joe, David, Frank? What kind of a person was he anyway? Dwelling on this was not good for his nerves. This he knew, yet he couldn't help it. It so sickened and enraged him. That his life should be poisoned by this single terrible act. Who did this to him? And how did other people manage their lives after such calamities? Were they so overburdened with hatred that their lives fell into ruins? Or were they able to face their futures? For it was certain that awful things happened every day. You read about them: drivers who didn't stop, drug-crazed teenagers who threw children off apartment building roofs, madmen who mutilated their victims and sent thumbs and ears in the mail, bodies stuffed into suitcases or left rotting in bus-station lockers. Thank God Jonathan had been intact. Farris poured another drink. But to be violated like that! The terror of it; the last suffocating moment. And whom did he cry out to? Who was there to listen? Trembling, Farris warned himself to be careful. He must stop thinking about the man and the crime; he must concentrate now on living. Jonathan was dead and no amount of wishing could restore his life. At least he was at peace, while his father must go on living.

He poured another large drink, assuring himself

that this would be the last. With an experienced drinker's cunning, he judged how many drinks were left in the bottle. The whiskey was now giving him a temporary feeling of triumph. He was about to experience the worst event in a person's life. After burying a child, nothing much can touch you. And he would survive.

Thinking about this, it crossed his mind that perhaps he should start again. Jonathan's death had surely broken the last bond between him and Pat, and it was foolish to imagine that they would ever get together again. She was stuck on this Neville; well, let her have him. So be it! This acceptance of his fate filled him with a kind of awe. Why shouldn't he break away, then? He could try another town. He could go to Calgary or Vancouver and catch on with a newspaper out there. It was not impossible. Craig would recommend him, and Craig's opinion was respected across the country. There was roughly fifteen hundred dollars in his account, and that was more than enough to stake him. He began to feel excited by the idea. He would throw everything out and get fresh clothes, right down to socks and underwear. And in a couple of weeks when all this was over, he'd cut down on the booze, maybe get back into shape with some sit-ups each morning. He would throw the cigarettes away, too. Christ, he was only forty-three. It would take a few days to settle everything, but no more. He'd sell the VW, close his account, and check out of this dump. To hell with his lease.

It struck him how simple it was to change your life if you really wanted to. Also, he would take the train west, no planes. Years ago he had traveled by train with the hockey teams, staying up all night to drink beer and play cribbage with the players. On a train you had time to think about where you were headed. He'd get a bedroom and put up his feet and sip whiskey while the country rolled past him. He'd pack about four bottles and some soda water. Once he got out there, he would stay sober and line up some interviews. He could already see himself answering an editor's questions. And people were bound to be sympathetic. His marriage had broken up, his son had been murdered, and he had to get away. He would show them Craig's recommendation and the two pieces he did for *Sports Illustrated*. Never mind that they were written a dozen years ago; he was still a professional, wasn't he?

He stood up and stretched his arms in front of him like a diver. They trembled slightly, but nothing people would notice. Standing there, he took the measure of his meager surroundings and was glad to be getting away. In the bedroom he laid out his clothes carefully and took his time dressing. His dark-gray suit was still presentable, and with it he would wear a soft blue shirt and maroon tie. Lifting a leg to the heating radiator by the window, he absently buffed a loafer with long hard strokes. But as he polished the shoe, he sensed a melancholy stealing over him, pushing aside his brief moment of confidence in the future. Twenty-five years ago on Friday nights he had leaned his leg just like this against the old radiators in his mother's house while polishing black shoes. Then, wearing draped charcoal-gray pants and a pink shirt, he had walked to Darlene's to talk about living together and loving each other for the next fifty years. And now he was halfway there. Farris seldom thought about his first wife anymore, though a few times a year he dreamed about her as she was in high school, a large-breasted girl with long brown hair. And thinking about her now, he was dismayed by the sadness attending the passage of time, the radical unhappiness at the heart of life.

After pacing back and forth a few moments, he decided on one last quick one before Pat arrived. In the kitchen he took it straight and afterward drank a glass of cold water. It seemed to restore and enlarge his spirits and, after washing his hands and face, he gargled Listerine and looked in the mirror. He was all right. Inside him the whiskey warmed and soothed, and he prayed it would last over the next couple of hours. He couldn't possibly risk taking a flask. At a quarter to two he locked his apartment door and walked down to the street where one of Robson's gray Cadillacs awaited him.

In the car Pat took his hand and squeezed it. Except for the driver, they were alone and Farris was glad. He guessed that Bill had insisted they go to the funeral as man and wife, and Pat still paid heed to her father's wishes. He was amazed at how beautiful she was even in mourning. Without speaking they held hands as the car turned east on Carlton toward Parliament Street. Along the sidewalk people stooped to see behind the tinted glass. When they turned north and approached the cemetery, he felt Pat's hand tighten. A crowd of a hundred or so were gathered on the sidewalk on either side of the gates, and across the street people in the St. James apartment buildings were looking down from their balconies. A TV van was parked against the curb in a no-parking zone and a huge cop was fiercely waving southbound traffic by the scene. Then he heard Pat say, "Charlie, I'm not sure I can take this. I may just blow it."

"Take it easy, now," he said, "it'll soon be over. The hard part's coming up and then it's over."

The big cop now stepped forward and waved them through the gates. Behind the dark glass Farris glimpsed faces in the crowd: a black man in work clothes, some teenage girls, an old crone dressed entirely in black with a kerchief on her head. She was Greek or Italian or Portuguese. She was weeping profusely. A TV man with a camera mounted on his shoulder focused on the Cadillac. Beside him Pat shuddered. How she loathed the crowd! He recalled how she wouldn't even stand in line for a movie ticket but preferred instead to sit inside the theater lobby.

In front of the chapel the circular drive was filled with cars, and from one of them emerged Bunny Buckley, his white soutane flowing in the breeze. Quickly he climbed the chapel steps and disappeared inside. Bill Langford helped his aged mother out of another car, and Teddy was there, too, lending a hand. Most of the men looked freshly barbered. Peter Neville stood to one side with his hands behind his back like a young naval attaché, darkly suited and good-looking. There were Langford cousins from Montreal and Boston, long-faced, middle-aged men and women who now climbed the stone steps to the chapel looking grave and proud. The driver parked in the remaining space behind the hearse and stepped out smartly to open the door on Pat's side. Once out of the car, Farris took her arm. Behind the veil she looked tranquil, though he knew she was fighting for some kind of control. As for him, there was now a headache. There was just too much nervous tension in his system and the whiskey seemed to have been burned out of his blood. Now he faced the chapel as sober as daylight. As they climbed the steps together he said, "Just take it about a minute at a time, Pat. Breathe deeply when you feel you're fading."

"I'm trying, Charlie." Her voice was so weak and

small that it frightened him. She sounded like an ailing child. Fifty yards behind them the crowd had scattered and surged forward against the iron fence for a better look. Farris was grateful that those people were not allowed inside the gates. How he had wished that today would be rainy and cold; that would have seemed more fitting. Instead it was a perfect sunlit afternoon. Overhead the pale sky was cloudless. The cemetery was beautiful too, though it had a worn, bare look to it this time of year. Over by the Bloor Street fence, workmen raked leaves into long windfall rows.

At the chapel door Tommy Robson greeted them in his dark coat and striped trousers. His tiny black shoes glistened in the sunlight that fell across the doorway. He nodded thoughtfully in their direction and passed them into the care of an usher who strode ahead of them down the aisle. The small chapel was half-filled and Buckley, looking sorrowful, stood by the pulpit waiting for them. Farris tried not to look at the casket and watched instead the woman seated at the small organ playing "Abide with Me." The old doleful tune brought sharp and painful memories to him. He hadn't heard it in years, and it brought to mind those childhood Sunday evenings when he had clutched his mother's hand as they left the Evangel Hall to walk home along the darkening streets of his hometown. Other children played games among the trees and in the shadows cast by the streetlight. But they stopped to watch Farris and his mother pass. And then, from a safe distance, they raised jeering voices calling out "Holy Roller" and "Jesus Jumpers." And in his bed he had cried for his violent, drunken soldier father, whom he remembered only vaguely, to return and protect him.

He had hated Sunday evenings ever since, and now

this tired banal hymn filled him again with loneliness and regret as they sat down in the front row directly ahead of Bill and his mother and Teddy and Sylvia. John Buckley addressed the altar with a slight bow and then turned to them. Farris could see that the priest was genuinely moved. He was a vain and pretentious man, but this was the burial service for an old friend's grandson who had been taken early. It was hard, perhaps impossible, to justify such a wicked deed. Buckley looked down at his shoes and then, raising his eyes, began to speak. Behind him Farris heard Lavinia Langford's breathy whisper. "That is John Buckley, isn't it? He's put on a great deal of weight since I last saw him. He's far too heavy." Beside her Bill Langford said, "Mother . . . please."

As Farris listened to Buckley, his mind was cast adrift. Words were meaningless. What could you say to such an outrage against decency? His son's death was beyond the comfort of words, however consoling. Behind him old Lavinia Langford now muttered curses, and to Farris they were just as intelligible as the priest's words. Next to him Pat stared ahead, rigid with grief. She was holding up well. And Buckley was doing his best. He spoke about God's will and the ultimate mystery of things. But did it not come down to this, thought Farris: Jonathan had been in the wrong place at the wrong time. Was it not largely a matter of bad luck? His mind again turned to the crime and he wondered about the man being held by the police. Was he the one? It sounded likely. But perhaps he wasn't! And if he wasn't, where was the person who did this terrible thing? Was he now in terrified hiding hundreds of miles away? Or was he just returning to work after his lunch? Farris tried to form a mental picture of the killer, but it was impossible. He could look like anyone; he might be anyone. He could be somebody's favorite uncle, or the nice young man down the street. With a soiled handkerchief Farris wiped his neck and brow and tried to follow Buckley's words. To his amazement he discovered that the service was nearly over and Buckley's arms were raised in benediction. *The Lord bless you and keep you. The Lord make his face to shine upon you, and be gracious unto you. The Lord lift up his countenance upon you, and give you peace, both now and evermore. Amen.* Buckley lowered his arms and turned once more to bow to the altar. Several people were sobbing, though Pat continued to stare ahead dry-eyed and erect. Her fists were clenched in her lap, and Farris covered them with his hand.

The organist began to play again and four of Tommy Robson's men stepped briskly forward and, grasping the coffin, carried it past the mourners. Farris breathed deeply. Now the hard part was about to begin. Behind them, Bill Langford cried openly and his old mother said, "Now, Willy, don't carry on so. He's been so sick. He's suffered so. Now he's out of his misery." Where was the old woman's mind now, wondered Farris. Was she thinking of her husband or her long-dead son Richard?

They followed the coffin up the aisle and through the doors into the bright November day. Along Parliament Street the small crowd still gaped through the iron railings. The Langford plot was on the north side of the cemetery, and soon cars were following the long gray hearse along the narrow driveway. As they passed, the workmen removed their caps and leaned on their rakes. At the graveside the mourners stood with bowed heads while Buckley read from his large prayerbook. The wind stirred the priest's hair and as he read he brushed it from his eyes. *I am the resurrection and the life, saith the Lord: he that believeth in me, though he were dead, yet shall he live: and whosoever liveth and believeth in me shall never die.* He paused and looked at the people over his half-moon reading glasses. *He shall feed his flock like a shepherd: he shall gather the lambs with his arm, and carry them in his bosom.* Around them were the weathered stones of Langfords long dead. And everyone must come to this, thought Farris as he gripped Pat's arm. A few feet away Peter Neville watched her with worried eyes.

And then Farris felt Pat go limp; her slack weight slipped against him and he seized her in both arms before she collapsed. Her face was sickly and colorless. Eyes closed, she whispered to him, "I can't make it, Charlie. I'm going to be sick. Take me back to the car." Buckley watched them and his voice faltered briefly, though he continued to read the service. People stepped aside as Farris half-carried his wife away from the graveside. Then Peter Neville was there to grasp Pat's other arm, and together they took her toward the car. Behind them Farris heard Lavinia Langford's voice: "Such a display. Whatever can be the matter with her?" And then Pat was sick. They reached the limousine and here she put out a hand for support and, leaning forward, vomited bile while the two men held her. When she had finished, Neville took out a handkerchief and carefully wiped her mouth. Farris opened the door and together they placed her on the wide seat. She pressed Neville's handkerchief against her eyes and Farris knew she was filled with shame. "I'm sorry," she said, "I'm so sorry." Neville held both her hands and talked softly to her. "It's all right, darling. Please don't worry about it. It'll soon be over." Looking at them, Farris realized with a kind of deadweight finality that a door on his life was closed forever. He touched Neville's elbow. "You better get in with her." The young man looked at Farris and then wordlessly climbed in beside Pat. Farris closed the door and, looking through the dark glass, saw his wife's averted stricken face. Her lover's arms were now around her.

When Farris walked slowly back to the graveside, the service was over. Jonathan's body had been lowered into the ground and Buckley was reading the last words. After he finished, people turned and quietly and eagerly headed for their cars. Some of them, Farris couldn't remember their names, squeezed his arm as they passed. A sad-eyed woman his own age raised herself on tiptoe to kiss him stiffly on the cheek. And Bill Langford, his face stark with grief, even a little wild-eyed, now brushed past a man and came across to Farris. "I want to drink a bottle of whiskey with you, Charlie."

"Not a good idea today, Bill," said Farris. "It just wouldn't work today." Langford blew his nose and wiped his eyes. He sounded furious. "Well, when then, goddamn it?"

"One day soon, Bill."

He had taken Farris's arm. "Listen, I don't want any of this 'one day soon' stuff." He looked around angrily. "I can't talk to any of these people, goddamn it." His light blue eyes were blazing. "I want you to come and see me. If Pat wants that Englishman, that's her business. You're my son-in-law and you always will be. You're Johnny's father, you helped to bring him into this world."

They heard Lavinia Langford calling out to them. "Willie, come along, I'm hungry."

Bill looked up at the leafless trees and blinked hard. He could never stay angry for long, and now his rage was spent. "I shouldn't have brought her. I thought she'd remember, but it was a mistake."

"It's all right, Bill," said Farris. "Look . . . go home and have two or three drinks. I'll phone you in a few days and we'll get together. . ."

Bill Langford placed both hands on Farris's shoulders and looked at him beseechingly. "Lord, I'm so confused, Charlie. This whole thing has just knocked me for a loop. I just don't understand how it could have happened. What did we do to deserve this, that's what I'd like to know." He shook his big head. "I'll tell you plain out, son, I'm confused. I just don't know what I'm going to do with the rest of my life." Farris said nothing and Bill shook him lightly and then pointed a forefinger. "You come and see me, Charlie. I'll hold you to that. I can't talk to these people."

"I will, Bill. I promise."

Langford shook Farris's hand awkwardly. "God bless you, Charlie." Teddy Langford hurried over to them. "Have you got a ride, Charlie?"

"No," Farris said, "but that's all right. I'm walking anyway. I want to walk."

"Are you sure?" asked Teddy. "We've got lots of room." His father looked irritable. "For heaven sakes, Ted, let him walk if he wants to."

Teddy looked confused. "Sure, Dad. No problem."

Farris said good-bye and waved to them as the large cars drove away. Pat and Neville had already left.

It was over at last. As he walked across the cemetery, he marveled at how one's life could change within a week. Last Monday at this time he was finishing lunch with Craig, who wanted him to write another hockey story. Farris was bored with hockey stories but needed the work, and Craig was convincing. A week ago Jonathan was at Germanfield Academy waiting for another weekend. Now everything was blasted. At the gate the crowd had dispersed and the TV crew was loading the van. Unnoticed, Farris crossed the road and walked westward along Howard Street in the shadows cast by the apartment buildings. The afternoon was cooling and he walked quickly. It took him just a few minutes to reach Sherbourne Street. A block away, he noticed the black Plymouth parked in front of his building. Grahame was alone, and he got out of his car as Farris approached. "Have you got a few minutes, Mr. Farris? I'd appreciate it."

"I need a drink," said Farris.

"Sure thing. It's a tough day for you. But this won't take long." In the elevator Farris studied the detective's face. The man looked very tired. "I hear you found the son of a bitch. Is that true?" asked Farris. Grahame gave the writer a sour look. "No," he said.

CHAPTER SEVEN

At the kitchen counter Farris poured himself a big shot and drank it off at once. Now he could get drunk. He had cigarettes and booze enough to last a few days. In the refrigerator there were things to eat if he felt like eating. He'd take the phone off the hook, turn on the TV, and try to forget for a while. Today he had lost his family. In the circumstances, a man was entitled to get drunk. Self-pity had its own rewards. By the window Grahame stood looking down at the street lost in thought. Either that or he was waiting for Farris to loosen up with whiskey. After his second drink Farris felt himself slowly relaxing. "My ex-wife said you arrested somebody." He added bitterly, "She seems to have a special pipeline right through to somebody."

Grahame shrugged. "He was a suspect briefly, but we had to let him go. Other than his record, we had nothing to hold him on."

"I thought he couldn't account for himself on Saturday night."

"That's what he said at first. But when he found

out why we were asking him questions, he soon told us where he was." The detective smiled grimly. "Would you believe it? This guy was shacked up on Saturday night with his parole officer's wife. He was banging the pants off her at the Chelsea Inn while her husband was out of town. She confirmed his story. It was embarrassing, but she confirmed it. Now all she has to do is explain it to her husband."

"So?" said Farris. He resented Grahame's comical little tale of infidelity. "You're now working on nothing. Right?"

"I wouldn't say nothing."

"I'm told the first forty-eight hours are crucial in these cases. After that the trail grows cold."

"Who told you that?" asked Grahame. Farris thought he detected a faintly insolent note in the question. But then cops were like doctors; they hated the idea that a layman might know something about their work. Farris sat down heavily. "I don't know. I guess I read it somewhere."

Grahame now sat down too and looked over at Farris. "We'll find them, Mr. Farris. Don't worry about that. It's only a question of time."

Farris looked up at him. "You said 'them.' Are you sure there was more than one person involved?" His heart beat thickly. They were now actually talking about Jonathan's killers.

"Yes, we are," said Grahame. "The pathologist has confirmed this by the 'bruises and contusions. . ."

"How bad were they?"

"Bad enough. Your son struggled. He put up a fight. At least two people were holding him. He was sexually assaulted, Mr. Farris. There was evidence of anal penetration."

"All right, all right." Farris closed his eyes. "Jesus fucking Christ, find them," he whispered. He accepted one of Grahame's cigarettes. "All right!" he said after a moment. "So there was more than one. That's really not so hard to figure out. I can't believe my twelve-year-old son would stand around and let himself be raped. . ." The awful word stuck in his throat. "Did you need a pathologist to figure that out?"

"Look, Mr. Farris," said Grahame, "sarcasm isn't going to help here. We've got a couple of hundred people out there working hard without much sleep. Everybody is doing a double shift on this. We don't like people who do this kind of thing and we want to find them."

"Fine. Okay . . . you're working hard. Great!" He sucked hard at his cigarette. Nowadays everyone felt obliged to offer a commercial on behalf of his efforts. "Have you not talked to people along this street and down along Carlton?" he asked. "Didn't anyone see Johnny last Saturday afternoon?"

"We've asked everybody within six blocks of here," said Grahame patiently. "Look, Mr. Farris, it's like this. People see but they don't take special notice. Why should they? They aren't looking for anything special. They're thinking about shopping or what they're going to do that night or whatever."

Farris got up for another drink. "But Christ Almighty, if a kid is pulled into a car or something. I mean, Jesus . . . somebody is going to see that . . . surely."

Grahame looked up at him. "Well, what makes you think Johnny might have been pulled into a car?"

Farris regarded his empty glass. "How the hell do I know? It's the kind of thing you read about in the papers, isn't it?" Grahame rose and followed Farris into the kitchen. "I don't suppose you can drink on the job, Sergeant?" asked Farris. The detective looked at the whiskey bottle and rubbed his neck. "I shouldn't, but it looks good. I'll take a very light one, Mr. Farris. Half an inch and lots of water." Farris took down a glass. "It's not worth pouring."

Grahame smiled. "Mr. Farris . . . if Johnny got into a car last Saturday, we don't think he was forced. *If* he got into a car . . . and we're not sure about that . . . but if he did, we think he got in willingly."

Farris took a deep breath. He didn't like the drift of this conversation. "What makes you think that? It doesn't sound like Johnny." He handed Grahame his drink. "Both my wife and me, we harped all the time about the danger of getting into strangers' cars. Johnny wasn't stupid; he knew the score. He knew what could happen to kids. We've told him about these things since he was a little boy of five or six." He swallowed another long, burning mouthful of whiskey.

"I believe you," said Grahame. "And after what you've told me, I'm convinced that Johnny knew the men who killed him."

"What are you saying exactly?" asked Farris. "That Johnny willingly got into a car and drove somewhere to be killed? That doesn't make any sense to me. How could he know such people, for Christ sakes? Where would he meet them, and why?"

"Those are good questions," said Grahame, sipping his drink, "and we are trying to find the answers. We have a theory about what might have happened."

"After two days a fucking theory. Great!"

"We have to start somewhere, Mr. Farris."

"Fine!"

For some reason they remained in the kitchen with Farris leaning against the counter and Grahame standing in the doorway. The detective explained. "In most sexually related homicides the victim knows the killer. To us it seemed unreasonable that a healthy twelve-year-old youngster could be abducted off a downtown street sometime between three and five o'clock on a Saturday afternoon without somebody noticing something. Nor did it seem reasonable, given what you and your . . . former wife have told us, that Johnny would have got into a car with strangers. Kids sometimes do this, but they're usually much younger, maybe five or six. So . . ." Grahame hesitated. "So one reasonable conclusion we can draw is that Johnny knew these people and had no reason to fear for his safety."

Farris drank again. "Then why for God sakes would these so-called acquaintances of his kill him?"

Grahame fished out another cigarette. "Who knows? Perhaps drugs were involved. Maybe somebody got high. Certain proposals were made and resisted. Things got a little out of hand. It wouldn't be the first time. When people are drinking or doping, anything can happen."

Farris shook his head in disbelief. "I can't buy it, Sergeant. How could Johnny know such people?"

Grahame finished his drink and put the glass back on the counter. "I drove down to your son's school this morning, Mr. Farris. I spent a couple of hours there."

"So?"

"It's a nice school. Beautiful grounds. The headmaster showed me around and we talked about Johnny. I also talked to some of the boys who knew him. What I really wanted to find out was what kind of a boy Johnny really was. You know, how other people saw him."

The whiskey had put things nicely out of focus for Farris, and now he knew that he could drink for several hours and maintain this fuzzy equilibrium. "And what did you find out, Sergeant?" he asked.

Grahame rubbed his neck again; it seemed a habit that preceded difficult questions. "How did you see your son, Mr. Farris?"

"What do you mean, how did I see him?"

"I mean, were you close to him? Was he a friendly kid? Did he confide in you much? That sort of thing."

Farris shrugged impatiently. What kind of questions were these anyway? "He was a twelve-year-old kid, Sergeant. Over the past year, since our marriage went bust, I only saw him on the weekends. And not every weekend either. In the summer we spent a week together."

Farris remembered that week as a disaster; he was simply not equipped to entertain a twelve-year-old for a whole week. They had gone to the movies and the Island and the Metro Zoo. But he sensed that Jonathan was bored; he'd seen all this before. And although the kid was too polite to say so, he would much rather have been up at the cottage waterskiing with his grandfather. Waterskiing was the big craze last summer. And there he was, stuck in hot Toronto with his beer-guzzling old man. That week was not a success and both of them were glad when it was over. Now Farris felt both guilty and indignant. He resented Grahame's prying questions. "His mother insisted on locking him up in that snotty private school. I didn't go for it, but she had custody. So I didn't see much of him. I'm a typical modern parent, Sergeant.

Loaded up to here with guilt." He chucked his flattened hand under his chin. "We fucked up everything, his mother and I... If our marriage had worked..." He turned away in disgust at the failures in his life. But Grahame persisted.

"Did you find Johnny, then ... withdrawn or moody when he visited you? Did you notice any abrupt changes in his mood?"

Farris turned to look at the detective. "What is this, Sergeant? The fucking child-psychology hour? When did cops start asking these kinds of questions? You sound like that psychiatrist fraud Toomey."

Grahame said nothing but looked down at the floor, and Farris felt ashamed. The man was only doing his job. "Well, I don't know," he said finally. "Kids are kids. I mean, sure he was moody at times. What kid isn't? It depended. But a twelve-year-old kid is going through all sorts of changes. It's a tough time for him. You have to expect moodiness."

The detective looked up at him. His gray eyes were dulled with fatigue. "Mr. Farris, did you know that Johnny was a regular user of marijuana?"

"Balls. The kid was only twelve years old."

"That's old enough. I've seen kids doping at eight or nine. It's not unusual."

"Well, I don't believe it," said Farris, though he wasn't at all so sure. There was no denying that Johnny had been a strange kid who enjoyed taking risks in life. Farris remembered one day last spring. It was just before he moved out of the house; the FOR SALE sign was already on the lawn. Alone in the house, Johnny got drunk on Farris's whiskey and threw up on the bathroom floor. Farris found him curled asleep around the toilet.

"We also know," continued Grahame, "that Johnny

was *selling* marijuana to kids at the school. Marijuana and other things."

"What other things?" asked Farris in a dull voice.

"Pornographic pictures," said Grahame. "I'm sorry I have to tell you this on the day of his funeral, Mr. Farris. But we found some of these pictures and some marijuana in Johnny's dorm at the school. Some of the boys have told the whole story."

"Sure they'd tell that kind of story. Johnny's dead now. He can't defend himself."

"Could you tell me if you or Mrs. Farris were in the habit of giving Johnny large sums of money?" These awful questions! Farris groaned aloud as he reached for the whiskey bottle.

"I haven't got large sums of money. His mother has, but she wouldn't give him money."

"What about his grandfather? I understand that Mr. Langford is pretty well off."

"Yes he is, but he wouldn't give Johnny money. Stereos, radio clocks, ten-speed bikes, things, Sergeant, expensive things. But not money. Not more than a few bucks, anyway. Why are you asking this?"

"Well, we found about three hundred dollars inside his mattress along with some dope and some of these pictures."

"The stuff could have been planted."

"Yes, it could have been, but we doubt it. The headmaster has had his suspicions for some time but has had nothing to pin them on. Apparently this has been going on for a few weeks now." He paused, but Farris said nothing. He was filled with such an angry bitterness that words failed him. On top of everything else was this revelation that his slain son might have been a criminal. Yet in his heart he knew it could be true. And when he thought more about it, the news was not all that surprising. Long ago he had sensed in his son that air of cool mockery toward authority and convention. At one time Farris had even admired it.

Now Grahame said, "We believe Johnny made these contacts, picked up the stuff, when he visited you. We also believe that it's these people who were selling him the stuff who killed him. Why they did is another question. Maybe the boy wanted to get out of it, and they got frightened that he would say something. We don't know that yet."

Farris felt tremendously burdened by all this. Pat had been right all along; if he'd lived in another neighborhood . . . He frowned at the detective. "How can you be so sure that he made these so-called contacts when he visited me?"

Grahame placed a small black pocket diary on the kitchen counter. "We found this in the mattress too, Mr. Farris. There are only the four entries. It looks like Johnny wrote them up on Sundays when he got back to the school."

Farris carefully examined his son's cramped and awkward handwriting.

October 12

Saw S. again yesterday. What a neat guy. He told me all about his childhood. Never knew his father and his mother was a hoor. He said when he was my age he had hitchhiked over half the States. He was very funny about some of his adventures. S. is about the funniest guy I know. He's so cool too. I like the way he walks around. He just seems to say the hell with you, this is how I'm going to do it. He also listens to you. Not like the Leprechaun though. The Leprechaun listens but you know he's trying to trick you into saying something meaningfull as he puts it.

Big deal. S. just listens because he's a friend.

October 19

It rained all weekend. Yesterday was one of the worst days of my life. Mother was in an evil mood. I couldn't do anything right. Of course Peter was there trying to be nice. She walks all over him. Why can't he see it? He does everything she says. Then the Leprechaun. I said nothing at all to him. Screw him. We spent an hour and I said nothing except hello, good-bye. It's a waste of time. I'm sick and tired of listening to him try to be funny. And that's it. People who aren't funny shouldn't try to be. Then Dad was grumping. Sat there sulking. Wanted to watch his jock shows I guess. Sometimes I feel I'm bothering him by being there. Yet he still wants me to come every week. Met S. later and went to a restaurant because it was pouring. Had coffee. S. doesn't bug me about ordering coffee. If it was Mother or Dad there would have to be a big deal. M. joined us after ten minutes. M. is ok, but a bit of a wimp. S. just orders him around and M. plays the faithful servant. A weird little guy. They invited me back to their place but I had no time. S's eyes were all glassy. He was really flying. Told me a story about an old man and his dog. Very funny but trés gross. I was late but Dad didn't notice.

October 26

It's funny. When you think something nice is going to happen, it doesn't and vice-versa. Like yesterday. I thought S. would be really happy because I had such a terrific week. A new sales record!!!!! Instead he was grumping. We sat on a bench and he hardly said a word. Sometimes he doesn't seem to care about anyone. I asked him about M. and he said nothing. It's funny how a friend can be so away from you even though you're sitting next to him. Mother and Peter had a quarrel later. I don't know what it was about but at least he stood up to her. But I felt kind of sorry for her when he did. Sometimes Mother looks old. Like tonight when she drove me to the station. I wish she and Dad still liked one another. At least then I wouldn't be in this cruddy place.

November 2
S. in much better mood yesterday. M. was there too following along like a little dog. S. wanted to know all about this place. How we slept and how many in a room and if guys did it in the showers or in their beds. He told me a couple of stories about prison life (I didn't know he'd been in prison). They were gross though I could see the same thing happening here maybe. We had a smoke and walked around. M. is not as much of a wimp as I thought. He listens to you. Wanted to know all about Mother and Dad and Peter. He said my life was like some TV program he watches every afternoon. Which I thought was funny in a way. Dad doesn't look very good. He seems to have lost some weight. I hope he doesn't have cancer or anything like that.

Farris's hands shook as he lit another cigarette. Grahame put the little diary in his pocket. "We'll keep this for a while, but I'll see that it's returned to you or the boy's mother." Farris shook his head as though to clear it. "I just don't see how he could have met such people."

It's easier than you think, Mr. Farris. From what I

can gather after talking to this Dr. Toomey and the headmaster of the school, Johnny was kind of a lonely kid. So maybe during one of these trips to the variety store a few weeks ago, he struck up a conversation with this S. character. And maybe this guy offered him a joint and maybe they went over to Allan Gardens and toked up. And, you know, it might have felt pretty good. That's why I asked you if you noticed anything different about him. But sometimes you know, a person can dope away and nobody will notice anything different about him. So after that, who knows? The point is, it's not that hard to fall in with those kind of people."

"I suppose not." Standing by the window, Farris looked down at the late-afternoon street. Despite the whiskey, his nerves were ragged. "Does his mother have to know about all this right now?"

"If she knows, maybe she can remember something that will help us."

"She's not well, Sergeant. She was sick at the funeral."

"I'm sorry, Mr. Farris."

At the door Grahame hesitated and then said, "If you can remember anything at all that you haven't told us about last Saturday, please give me a call."

The door closed and a moment later Farris picked up the ringing telephone to hear the voice of a woman he didn't recognize. "Are you the Mr. Farris who lost his little boy?" she asked. The voice was elderly. "I lost my son Billy in a car accident thirty years ago this January. You never get over it. But you have to remember what our Lord said, Mr. Farris. 'Suffer the little children to come unto me, and forbid them not: for of such is the kingdom of God.' Mark 10. Verse 14. Our church puts out a pamphlet to parents whose children have passed away. It's been printed up in the *Reader's Digest*. I can send you . . ." Farris hung up and then took the phone off the hook. For a moment he couldn't remember what day of the week he was living through.

CHAPTER EIGHT

Walking steadily though quite drunk now, Farris left his apartment clutching a bottle of Gordon's gin. In the hallway he saw Mr. Hassan, who was standing by the elevator holding his soft leather briefcase against his chest. Mr. Hassan, a short, serious bachelor from Pakistan, nodded curtly at Farris and entered the elevator on his way to another evening class in psychology or human relations. Fuck you too, buddy, Farris muttered to himself. Mr. Hassan worked as a janitor for the Transit Commission, but he was hoping for better things. When Farris first moved into the Del Monte Arms, Hassan had visited him carrying two bottles of lager. They sat in Farris's living room and talked. Mr. Hassan believed in education and the future of Canada, but there was much to be overcome in this country in the field of human relations. As he talked, he made himself a sandwich from assorted meats in Farris's refrigerator. Canadians, lectured Hassan, were good people, but a trifle lazy and not altogether above prejudice. Dark-skinned people were not always welcome, hence they must constantly exercise control. Control was the key, and that was why he took courses in psychology and human management. Nor was he destined to spend the rest of his days sweeping down subway platforms. Farris grew increasingly tired of his new neighbor's complaints and suggested that many immigrants were touchy and vain and imagined prejudice where it did not exist. Mr. Hassan resisted this argument, and after a while the two men began actively to dislike each other. Shouts were exchanged and the immigrant left in a dignified huff, taking with him his half-eaten meat sandwich and the two empty lager bottles. The two neighbors now appeared to be enemies.

Farris paused in front of Mrs. Farnsworth's door and tried to summon forth an air of goodwill. Meeting Mr. Hassan in the hallway had briefly put him in an ill temper. But then Mr. Hassan and his prickly manner could go to hell; Mrs. Farnsworth was a good old soul and here he was to return her bottle with genuine gratitude. From inside came the sound of the television weatherman with his prediction of showers and isolated snow flurries in the suburbs. It would grow colder by the end of the week and this Indian summer would be over. Farris could hear also the clatter of dishes and cutlery. The old girl was probably eating her dinner, and he debated whether he should return another time. But he decided to knock on the door, and a moment later it opened on its chain and Farris stared in at one of Mrs. Farnsworth's mildly glazed eyes. "Who is it?" she asked and then recognized him. "Why, Mr. Farris!"

Farris bowed slightly and held up the gin bottle. "Good evening, Mrs. Farnsworth, I'm returning your gift." She undid the chain and opened the door. "Well, you certainly didn't have to do that, Mr. Farris. It wasn't necessary at all. Please come in." She stepped aside, and Farris walked into the warm, airless apartment. He had been here briefly only once before, to borrow a light bulb. The remains of Mrs.

Farnsworth's evening meal were on a small table in front of the color TV, and she seemed embarrassed at having been caught out like this. Yet Farris imagined that she ate most of her meals in front of the television. He had given her the gin and so now, still holding the bottle, she turned off the TV. They both watched the bright screen splutter into darkness. "I was just having some tea, Mr. Farris. Please sit down. Can I get you something?" She was clearing away the dishes, moving about with the quick precise zeal of a small person. Farris sat down in a large brown leather chair, and she asked again if there was something she could get him. She suggested a small gin and he nodded stiffly. "That would be fine, Mrs. Farnsworth." He thought he sounded like a clergyman out for a visit and he wondered if this heavy courtliness disguised his intemperance. He heard her in the kitchen casting about for ice and mix and he felt dizzy, almost sick. He'd already drunk too much too quickly and he didn't really need another drink in this hot stuffy place. He should have asked for tea.

To steady his mind, he concentrated on Mrs. Farnsworth's apartment. It had a similar layout to his, but it was much better furnished and she had cleverly used one part of her living room as a dining area. Her furniture had been brought out from England. It was old-fashioned and looked expensive. Probably it reflected her soldier husband's taste. Farris guessed he was now sitting in the major's reading chair. Mrs. Farnsworth had this peculiar marital arrangement whereby she lived alone in the Del Monte Arms for most of the year but joined her retired husband for several winter weeks in Portugal. The major chose to live in Sussex during the rest of the year; he had tried Canada for a while but couldn't abide the place. His wife, on the other hand, liked

Toronto, and once a year she also visited an old school friend in Victoria, British Columbia. Farris had heard all this from the superintendent's wife, who had related the story with evident envy.

Mrs. Farnsworth had mixed him an enormous martini, which she now offered on a tray. "Will you join me, Mrs. Farnsworth?" asked Farris, taking the cold glass. She looked confused by the suggestion, wondering perhaps whether it looked right to drink a cocktail so soon after dinner. Nevertheless, she was persuaded and soon came in with her drink to sit opposite Farris. The martini was excellent: dry and potent and light after the heaviness of the whiskey. Farris guessed his neighbor had mixed thousands of these marvelous drinks. As she sipped her martini, she seemed to brighten; there was fresh color in her cheeks. Staring across at her, Farris said, "I'm drunk, Mrs. Farnsworth."

She smiled. "No you're not, Mr. Farris. That's simply not true. You're not drunk at all. I've seen plenty of drunken men in my time, Mr. Farris, and you're not drunk."

"Yes I am," said Farris stubbornly. "Not stupid drunk maybe, but drunk all the same."

Mrs. Farnsworth considered this for a moment and then said, "Well, you're certainly not objectionable and I think that's what matters. Some men can hold their liquor and others can't. I refuse to believe that you would ever be objectionable. You've always struck me as a gentleman."

Farris stared between his knees at the empty glass, remembering all the times when in fact he had been perfectly objectionable: the parties ruined and afterward the scenes with Pat. "Well, my wife never thought I was a gentleman, Mrs. Farnsworth. She thought I was often crude and uncivilized. And she was right." He knew his remark was virtually unanswerable, yet Mrs. Farnsworth smiled again and said, "I'm sure that's not true."

"Oh, it's true, Mrs. Farnsworth. It's true enough." What was he trying to say about Pat? He couldn't remember. Had he buried his son only hours before? Was his wife at this moment in the arms of her lover? "Can I have another drink, Mrs. Farnsworth? I'd appreciate it." As if glad of something to do, she sprang from her chair. "Why certainly, Mr. Farris."

"My wife . . ." he began. He seemed to be talking to himself. "She never understood. . ." What was there to understand? In his own ears he sounded like some tiresome bar drunk, yet he couldn't help talking. "I disappointed her, I suppose. After my book came out and it wasn't a big success, she lost interest in me. It's a terrible thing to say, but it's the truth. She just lost interest." None of that was true. Why was he saying such things? Something in the recesses of his brain dimly told him that he was on his way to being disastrously drunk. Mrs. Farnsworth had returned with two brimming glasses. As she stood above him, he thought that her small pretty face looked flushed. He decided she was tippling in the kitchen and he was sympathetic; he knew that old trick.

She handed him one of the glasses. "I knew you were some sort of journalist, Mr. Farris, but I didn't know you were an author."

"Yes," said Farris, "I did write a book once. I wrote it in England, Mrs. Farnsworth. We lived over there, you see. For about a year. My son was three years old at the time." He had forgotten his cigarettes, and now he asked Mrs. Farnsworth if she smoked, though he saw no ashtrays in the place. Still, she produced from a drawer some stale Craven A's, which she said she kept for guests. This gesture deeply touched Farris and he felt suddenly expansive toward the little woman. "What a perfect hostess you are, Mrs. Farnsworth! I mean, that's fantastic. Keeping cigarettes for guests when you don't even smoke. And I'll bet you hate the smell of them."

"Oh no . . . not true, Mr. Farris," she said. "I don't mind the smell of cigarette smoke at all. Gerald used a pipe for years, though he gave it up some time ago. . ."

They fell into silence until he heard her ask him what his novel was about. It was always the question people asked. What is your book about? And it was such a difficult question to answer. It had taken him a year to write; he knew that. And in it he had tried to capture the sounds and sights and smells of his unhappy childhood. But why he had taken a year of his life to revive those old bad memories would remain forever a mystery to him. In any case the book was a failure; the only truly convincing character was his thin, anxious mother with her Bible and her air of helplessness. When his father returned from the Army, he took one look at his wife and child and fled to his drinking companions, never to return. A man very like him died in a Vancouver flophouse years later. After that, Farris's mother boarded the traveling evangelists who preached at the Evangel Hall. Farris would always remember those strange pilgrims, especially the huge bald-headed black man named Sunny Jim Hopkins. Each morning he sang hymns while he shaved his long cheeks. After breakfast he placed nine-year-old Farris on his knee and told him Bible stories. And there was the handsome young man who drank rum in his room before going forth to preach. In the late afternoon Farris and his mother sat with their guests in the dining room, which smelled of sour furniture polish. And there his mother served them fried bread and beans and canned peaches. Sometimes she bought a cream pie from Sunshine Bakeries.

But what the book was really about Farris couldn't say. Certainly it had not sold many copies, though the publisher didn't seem worried by this. "Wait until your next one," he said. "Let's have lunch and talk about it." And they did have lunch a few times over the next couple of years. But then the second book never came, and at some point they stopped having lunch. Only a year ago Farris had seen this man at a party launching the autobiography of a moronic young hockey player. But the publisher, now thicker around the waist and grayer, had looked away in embarrassment, and Farris had the strong impression that the publisher was trying to remember Farris's name.

Now he was aware that Mrs. Farnsworth was again somewhere in the kitchen. What was she doing? Mixing drinks? Had he fallen asleep for a moment? He called out to her. "My novel was about my childhood, Mrs. Farnsworth." He seemed to have spoken too loudly, for she came in and stood near the dining area and looked at him. "I see. . . Perhaps I could get it from the public library."

"Oh, I wouldn't bother if I were you, Mrs. Farnsworth," he said. "It's not a very good book. I can see that now. I'm a good journalist, but no novelist. My wife was right to be disappointed." Standing there, she seemed not to be listening. "I started a novel once." She laughed thinly. "When Gerald and I were in India just after the war. The days were so long and hot that I used to write away in a notebook in a little room shaded by a huge tree. In the middle of the day it was the only cool place. And everyone else was resting while I scratched away." There was another small laugh. "It was a very romantic story, Mr. Farris. All about a young WAC who meets her hero and goes abroad. I never finished it, I'm afraid. . ."

Farris wasn't listening. He had finished his drink and sat looking at the empty television screen. "I buried my son today, Mrs. Farnsworth," he announced. She hurried to his side and, drawing a chair closer, took his hand. He could smell gin and the faint elderly odor of lilac sachet. He dropped his head back against the chair and shut his eyes against the tears. "It's hard, Mrs. Farnsworth," he said. "It's very hard. You see, I want to smash something. . ." She was patting his hand. "Now, Mr. Farris, please. . ." She paused and looked away. "It must be very hard. Gerald and I never had a child, though I wanted one very badly." Was she weeping? Farris couldn't be sure. But wasn't it despicable for him to be in here crying in front of this sixty-year-old woman? Why had he not just delivered the gin and returned to his apartment? "I better go," he said, "it's getting late."

"Oh, do have one more drink, Mr. Farris," she said. "I don't get much company."

"I'm not very good company," muttered Farris.

"Yes you are," she said. "You are very good company. And what's more, you're a handsome and intelligent young man and you're bearing a terrible tragedy. You mustn't say that you aren't good company. You must let me be the judge of that. Now . . . we're going to have another drink. Just a little one." Again she patted his hand, and Farris realized that his neighbor was also drunk. He himself felt leaden, and he badly needed another cigarette. He couldn't be certain what time it was and it seemed an effort to look at his watch. Then he and Mrs. Farnsworth were sitting on the sofa and she was stroking his hair like a lover. She called him Charlie, too, though he couldn't remember giving her his first name. Perhaps he had fallen asleep again for a few minutes. Yes, he could have been sitting here asleep like an old man. Mrs. Farnsworth held his hand and crooned in his ear. "Now, Charlie, everything is going to be all right." When he turned, her face was a mere blur, the features melting and dissolving. "Nothing will ever be all right again, Marjorie," he said. When had he started calling her Marjorie? There was a part of this evening that was lost forever.

"Try not to think about it, dear. Give it time." He could taste lipstick. Had he kissed this old woman?

"I think I must have fallen asleep," he said. "Sorry. I'm drunk, you see."

"A little tipsy, dear. Nothing to worry about."

"Did I snore there? I think I did."

"A little, perhaps. Not to worry."

"I need a cigarette." He searched again through the empty package. "I have to go back to my apartment. Find some cigarettes. What time is it?"

Mrs. Farnsworth peered at her tiny wristwatch, holding it close to her eyes. "It's nearly ten o'clock, dear. It's not very late."

"Christ! Have I been here that long? I don't remember."

"Come along now. Let's get you some cigarettes." To his amazement he realized that she was going to accompany him. Had he invited her back to his apartment? For the life of him he couldn't remember doing so.

Getting up from the sofa seemed to require an enormous effort. He was vaguely aware of Mrs. Farnsworth standing over him and tugging at his arms. But then she lost her grip and fell gently backwards to the rug. As she fell he caught sight of a narrow thigh and long white bloomers. She giggled. "Oh dear, this is terrible. I slipped."

Farris reached out for her. "Here, let me help you." He bent forward to pull her up, but it was impossible and finally he, too, sat down beside her on the rug. There he put his arm around her while she tightly grasped his hand. "Oh dear," she said, without much conviction. "What a state we're in, Charlie!"

Her face was only inches away, yet to Farris it was indistinct. "Yes," he mumbled stupidly, and she touched his cheek with warm fingers. "Dearest Charlie... Your poor dear man, we must get you some cigarettes. Come along now."

With difficulty they rose and arm in arm lurched toward the door and out into the hallway. Farris thought it would be a fine joke of Hassan should see them staggering around. And outside her door he stopped to surge unsteadily against her. "What do you think of that Mr. Hassan?" he asked. "Is he not a"—he searched for words—"a stuff shirt . . . a pompous little fart? I don't like that man, Marjorie . . . I'll tell you that for a fact. I could kick his brown arse and probably will if I see . . ." But Mrs. Farnsworth pulled him along. "Now . . . now . . . never mind poor Mr. Hassan. We don't care about Mr. Hassan..."

"*HASSAN,*" bellowed Farris at the empty hall before Mrs. Farnsworth pushed him through his apartment doorway. Once inside, with the door closed, they both laughed. It was as though they had pulled some immensely intricate joke on the rest of humanity. "We must have a drink, Margie," said Farris. "I think a little drink . . . will put us in the pink." He laughed delightedly.

"Whatever you say, Charlie," said Mrs. Farnsworth, who was casually inspecting his apartment, supporting herself like a blind person by grasping the tops of chairs and tables. Farris found his cigarettes and poured two large whiskeys. In the living room something crashed and the light shifted. On her knees by the window, Mrs. Farnsworth groped for a fallen lamp. The bulb was smashed and something was sputtering. With elaborate care Farris crossed the room and, bending forward, pulled the plug from the wall socket. On her hands and knees, Mrs. Farnsworth was softly weeping. "Here. Don't worry about that now," he said, patting her shoulder. "It's only a goddamn lamp. It's nothing at all." Mrs. Farnsworth got to her feet and cautiously made her way to the sofa. She appeared to have been dealt a colossal insult, and on the sofa she stared ahead without looking at him. "Charlie, please don't swear," she said finally. "I can't abide a man who uses foul language. It is one of Gerald's good points. He never swears. About the worst he'll say is 'bloody' and I've grown used to that. But I don't like blasphemy, Charlie."

Farris handed her a glass of whiskey. Without knowing why, he felt affronted. "All right. . . You made your point. Drink up."

"Thank you, Charlie," she said, taking the glass in both hands. They sat on the sofa, wordlessly sipping the whiskey and listening to the traffic passing under the window. An abeyant melancholy had seeped into their evening together, and Farris drunkenly took note of this change in atmosphere. "I'm going to put on some music," he said, getting up and walking stiffly to his record player. The labels were a blur, and settling the needle on the spinning disc was a vexation to him. But soon they were listening to Artie Shaw's old band playing "Begin the Beguine." He remembered lying in bed as a child listening to this music. On Saturday nights it drifted across the town from the Starlite Dance Pavilion. And below him his mother sat on the veranda in the warm summer evenings and rocked and knitted. She was still a young woman; younger than he himself now was. Farris's heart was suddenly filled with feeling and he opened his arms to Mrs. Farnsworth. "Come on . . . let's dance . . . little lady." To his horror, he couldn't remember her name. It was either Margaret or Marjorie.

Farris held her tightly against him, and they shuffled about the room in a large, slow circle. Leaning against him, Mrs. Farnsworth murmured in his ear, "I haven't danced in years. Gerald and I used to go to the Officers' Club every Saturday night when we were first married. All those young men in their uniforms! They were so handsome." Farris barely listened to her. When he thought of his wife and dead son, he was filled with shame. What kind of a man would dance drunkenly with a stranger on the night of his son's funeral? Mrs. Farnsworth reached for his hand and laid it against her chest. They kissed one another and, astonished, he felt her thrust her groin upward against him. Then he was aware of clothes on his bedroom floor, and he stepped around them to touch Mrs. Farnsworth, who stood before him pale and thin in her slip. His shoulder ached and he seemed to remember falling against the doorjamb on his way into the bedroom.

Farris drew Mrs. Farnsworth down to his soiled bed and there they embraced. Her small, dry body was a torment to him, and so too was the crooning in his ear. A feeling of utter helplessness swept over him, and exhausted, he lay back and stared at the ceiling. Mrs. Farnsworth's head now rested on his chest, and he thought she was asleep until she lifted his limp member. But soon he felt himself being borne away; he saw his dead son's angry face in the coffin, and after a moment, like a miracle, he fell into the dark mercy of sleep.

PART TWO

CHAPTER ONE

At eleven-thirty on the Friday following his son's funeral, Farris received a telephone call about the murder. He hadn't bothered to change his number, and in fact all week had received only three calls, two from old friends who offered sympathy and one from Craig about a job. Now he was on his way to a luncheon meeting with Craig after a week in which he had done no work and indeed had been barely sober. When he wasn't drinking, he walked the gray downtown streets, staring with hostility at the faces of passersby. Until they discovered his son's murderer, every man was his enemy.

The story of the murder had now faded from the front page, but Farris was condemned to remember. And so his dreams were filled with terrifying images of his son's last moments. At three o'clock in the morning he would awaken and in his pajamas stand by the window smoking and drinking whiskey. At such times he also considered the years that lay ahead of him. He might write another hundred stories about jockeys and lady wrestlers, and he would probably write them with an ailing liver in places like the Del Monte Arms. When he died, his neighbors would notice the smell. And thinking of his neighbor, he flinched at the memory of their evening together. Since then they had avoided each other, and he had the distinct impression that Mrs. Farnsworth was in hiding behind her door, waiting for him to go out. And so at eleven-thirty on this cloudy Friday he put on his coat and stood in his kitchen finishing his third whiskey. When the telephone rang, he debated whether he should drink the last inch in the bottle. "Yes? What is it?" he asked.

"Mr. Farris? Mr. Charles Farris?" It was a young man's voice, but it was light and nervous.

"Yes."

"Are you the man whose little boy was killed last weekend?"

"Yes, I am," said Farris slowly. He would give the caller a chance. After all, he might just want to express his feeling of outrage or sympathy for another person's suffering. It was amazing how a little whiskey could make you feel so benevolent.

"Mr. Farris," the high, thin voice began, "please don't hang up. What I'm going to say will sound bizarre, but believe me, I'm not crazy and I'm not lying. But I know who killed your little boy."

Here it was, then, thought the writer. An authentic crank at last. He supposed one had to expect this sort of thing. Farris said, "If you know who killed him, you had better tell the police. Okay? Good-bye." He prepared to hang up, but the caller spoke hurriedly. "Wait—please, Mr. Farris. Don't hang up on me. I can't go to the police."

"Why not?" asked Farris. He had picked up the whiskey bottle and now he hefted it in his hand. Was a man who was being harassed by cranks not entitled to another drink, even at eleven-thirty in the morning? Farris cradled the phone in his shoulder and worked off the top of the bottle. He heard his caller breathing, and then the voice said, "I just can't go to the police, that's all." Farris swallowed some of the whiskey, holding the bottle by the neck.

"They would beat me," said the caller. More than likely, thought Farris. But what was this guy getting at? What was his game? "Listen," said Farris. "If this is a joke, it's in fucking bad taste." He tried to picture the man behind the voice; he sounded more like a youth. Was he just some harmless little guy sitting in his underwear in a YMCA room?

"I'm sorry, Mr. Farris," said the caller. "I didn't have anything to do with it, believe me. I just know who did, that's all. And I'm frightened, Mr. Farris. I'm really scared." Farris finished the whiskey. Who needed this melodrama anyway?

"All right. Okay. I'll play the game. Who killed him?"

"Mr. Farris, I'm not going to tell you that over the telephone."

"Of course you're not. We're going to meet on the merry-go-round at the amusement park. Or in a dimly lit bar. I've seen that movie too."

"Amusement park?" The voice sounded puzzled. "I don't know what you're talking about, Mr. Farris. I do want to meet you, though. It's very important."

"Right."

"I need some money, Mr. Farris." Farris looked at the empty bottle with disgust. He could have easily thrown it through the front window.

"You miserable bastard," he whispered and placed the phone on the hook. The call had soured his day. When he awakened that morning, he had looked forward to seeing Craig again. In his own way the magazine editor could be an amusing man. Now Farris wasn't sure he wanted to hear any of Craig's stories. Searching in the cupboards under the sink, he found, in a dusty bottle behind a can of cleanser, an inch or two of Bols gin. The stuff had been there since he moved in. On that warm, murky night he sat on his suitcases in the middle of the empty, freshly painted living room drinking Pimm's Cup, the uprooted middle-aged male, angry and frustrated as an old bear who has seen a tree fall suddenly across the entrance to his cave. Now he tasted the thick syrupy drink and listened as the phone again rang. He drank some of the syrup, but the phone wouldn't stop ringing. Farris picked up the receiver, reminding himself to get in touch with the phone people later in the day.

"All right," he said calmly, "is it you again? Now what exactly do you want from me?"

"Yes," said the voice. "Look . . . Mr. Farris. I *know* who killed Johnny. But I need help. I'm frightened."

There was a long silence and then the stranger said, "I can tell you some things about Johnny and Mrs. Farris and Peter."

"What things?"

"Johnny didn't like Peter very much, did he?"

"Peter who? What are you talking about?"

"Mr. Neville. Peter Neville. Johnny didn't like him. He was scared that Peter would become his stepfather." Farris's heart now beat quickly. It was very odd indeed to hear this kind of talk from a stranger.

"I'm only telling you this," said the voice, "so you'll know I'm no fake. Johnny used to tell all this to a friend of mine. Johnny didn't like Peter's things . . . his clothes and shoes and stuff . . . in his mother's apartment. I understand Peter used to leave a change of clothes in Mrs. Farris's apartment. And Johnny didn't like that. It upset him, according to my friend. He once set fire to a pair of Mr. Neville's pajamas."

A wave of anxiety passed through Farris. His scalp tingled and he felt himself perspiring. There *had* been an incident a few weeks ago. On the telephone Pat had mentioned something about Johnny setting fire to some of Peter's things one weekend. Apparently he used the bathtub. But she hadn't mentioned what things: only that the boy was becoming increasingly unmanageable and irritable and would Farris talk to him about other people's property. Characteristically, Farris had forgotten. But how could this stranger know about that unless he'd known Johnny? He thought now about the diary and recalled what Grahame had said about the boy probably knowing his killers. "Did you know my son?" he asked.

"No, Mr. Farris, I never knew Johnny. I just heard all about him. He told my friend everything."

"All right, all right," said Farris. "Look . . ." His hands felt clammy on the telephone. "Let's get on with this. What do you know? And how much do you want?"

"Mr. Farris, I want to leave town. I have to leave town, but I'm broke. I want to get so far away from Toronto that no one here will ever see me again."

"What's the matter? Are you in trouble with the police?"

"No. It's not the police. But there may be people looking for me. I'm not sure, but I think there may be."

"Okay. What people?"

"Just people."

"Are they the people who killed my son?"

"I'm not saying anything over the phone, Mr. Farris."

It was hard to believe this was happening. Farris swallowed hard.

"All right. You want to get out of town. I want to find out who killed my son. Where do we go from here?"

"I need a one-way ticket to Vancouver and one thousand dollars."

"That's very cheap. I would have thought the going rate for extortion was much higher these days."

"Mr. Farris, I am *not* a criminal." The voice now seemed more assured, almost petulant. "I am not joking about this."

"All right, you're not joking. It's just that it's hard to believe, that's all." How he wished he could keep liquor in the place. He badly needed another drink.

"I've told you about Johnny resenting the presence of your wife's lover in the apartment. I know all about your marriage breakup. Johnny was a very unhappy kid... He told my friend everything." Farris hated hearing this from a stranger.

"Did your friend kill him?" he asked sharply.

"I'm not going to say anything more over the phone, Mr. Farris."

"Look, whoever you are," said Farris. The whole thing was exasperating. "This is incredible. Ridiculous. Where can we meet?"

"Do you have a car?"

"Yes."

"What kind?"

"A Volkswagen bug. Dark blue."

"License number?"

Feeling foolish, Farris gave him the license number. All along he had been trying to study the voice. The caller sounded young and faintly effeminate. He listened carefully as the caller spoke again.

"There are seats still available on tonight's nine o'clock flight to Vancouver. It's Canadian Pacific

Flight 324. I want you to buy a one-way ticket in the name of Donald Howard and get one thousand dollars in cash."

"Small bills, of course," said Farris sarcastically, but the young man ignored his tone.

"Yes. Small bills. Bring the ticket and money with you, and pick me up at the southeast corner of Yonge and Dundas at seven o'clock and drive me to the airport. I'll tell you everything in the car."

"That sounds easy enough. I can manage that. Will you be alone?"

"Yes. That's the southeast corner, Mr. Farris. Near the bookstore."

"I know the corner," said Farris. "How will I recognize you?"

"Just drive to Dundas and Yonge. Go north on Yonge and stay in the right lane. If the light is red, you'll have to stop, of course, and I'll get in. If the light is green, just slow down a little and I'll tap the window on the passenger's side. Remember to keep the passenger door unlocked."

"All right. I've got that. At seven I drive slowly north on Yonge in the curb lane. At the corner you'll get in the car."

"Correct." The voice hesitated. "You'll probably be tempted to tell the police about this. I suppose that's only natural. But if you do, I will deny everything. Remember, I had nothing to do with Johnny's death. You have to believe that, Mr. Farris. All I ask is that you give me eight hours. I just need eight hours. And then you can tell the police everything. Do I have your word?"

"My word?"

"Yes," said the young man. "I think you're an honest man, Mr. Farris. I've read some of your articles even though I personally loathe sports. But I think you're honest. Do I have your word, then, that you won't inform the police about any of this until eight hours after I tell you everything?" Farris was thinking how Jack Grahame would love to be asking this young man questions.

"Well, eight hours is a long time," said Farris. "Johnny's killer could be long gone by that time. I guess he probably already is."

"They aren't going anywhere," said the voice. "They are staying in one place."

Farris now held the slippery phone in both hands. "You said 'they.' There was more than one, then?"

"I'm not saying anything more. Do I have your word? Eight hours?"

"Yes. All right." Farris was thinking of what Grahame would say to all this.

"Swear it."

"What?"

"Swear that you won't tell the police until eight hours after I tell you everything?"

"All right, I swear that I won't tell the police."

"Until eight hours after—"

"Okay, okay." Farris repeated the words, then added, "What's your name anyway?"

"Donald. Make the ticket out to Donald Howard."

"Okay, Donald."

"Please don't treat this as a joke, Mr. Farris. It's very important."

"You can't blame me for being a little skeptical."

"How could I know anything about Johnny and your wife's lover and all the rest of it?" The voice now sounded peevish.

Farris said slowly, "I don't know."

"I'll see you tonight, Mr. Farris. And please remember: if you want to know who killed Johnny, you must cooperate with me."

"All right, it's a deal. Yonge and Dundas at seven."

"Good-bye, Mr. Farris. I'm sorry about all this. My friend told me what a nice kid Johnny was."

"Yeh. Right." Farris hung up feeling oddly elated. Perhaps the guy was a crackpot, but why take chances? Immediately he dialed Grahame's number. His word! Who the hell gave his word to creeps like that? If this guy was for real, Grahame could follow them in his car. He guessed a man like Grahame would soon find out whether the guy was telling the truth or not. And yet the young man seemed to know all about Johnny's so-called family. It followed, then, that if he hadn't known Johnny, he must know someone who did. Farris felt uncomfortably perplexed. When the call went through, he asked for Sergeant Grahame. But he was told that Grahame was not there. Was there any message? Farris hesitated. He didn't think so.

CHAPTER TWO

On his way down to Chinatown he thought about the telephone call. He felt almost weak with excitement. For the first time in days, he looked forward to something. Meantime, there was this meal with Craig and perhaps that also would be a good thing. Lately he had been alone too much.

Craig loved the Canton Tea Gardens on Dundas Street. He had eaten lunch there for years, and the waiters knew him and fussed over him. After parking his Volkswagen in an elevated lot near University Avenue, Farris descended to the windy, gray street now thronged with noonday office workers hurrying to stores and restaurants. Ahead of him, a half block away, he saw Craig in a tweed overcoat and deerstalker. At six and a half feet, he easily towered over everyone. His back was toward Farris and he was opening the restaurant door for a young woman. At least, Farris assumed it was a young woman, and knowing Craig, it had to be, for womanizing was his hobby and vice. He liked young women, and the younger the better. He once told Farris how he seduced his sixteen-year-old daughter's best friend at the summer cottage. His wife seemed to tolerate this philandering. She was a tall forlorn-looking lesbian who had inherited a fortune and spent a great deal of time serving on various committees associated with her daughters' school. She also played a strong game of tennis, and during the winter months went south alone to compete in amateur tournaments. And, according to Pat, have a fling with the girls. The Craigs lived in a comfortable old house near Upper Canada College, only a few blocks from Bill Langford's.

For some reason Farris was thinking of Edna Craig when he entered the restaurant. Craig was already seated at a corner table in conversation with the young woman. Farris guessed she was in her early twenties, a brunette with a strong, intelligent face. She wore jeans and denim shirt with a striped suit coat. On the seat beside her lay a man's flat cloth cap. When he was standing over them, Craig looked up, his blue eyes huge behind the thick tortoiseshell glasses. "Charlie! You're on time for a change. Welcome. Look, I've brought along a guest. This is Madeline Greene. Mady, meet Charlie Farris. I've told you about his stuff. This man is a professional." The girl looked up from the menu and nodded at Farris without smiling. Another one of these tough, cool bitches, he thought. He wasn't sure he would like her. Craig was a talker, and when it came to Chinese food, a knowledgeable braggart. He ordered for the three of them.

The restaurant was noisy and crowded with the waiters hurrying by, holding aloft great platters of food. From this corner table Craig surveyed the scene. This was his turf and he always felt magnanimous here. He seemed in no hurry to discuss

Farris's new assignment; instead he mostly talked to the girl about Chinese cooking. Half-listening, Farris nursed his scotch and thought about the phone call. He had decided to meet this joker, though the price of a plane ticket and a thousand dollars would just about clean out his account. He hoped Craig was carrying an advance in his pocket, though Craig hated discussing money. But then people who had plenty of it usually did. The girl seemed to be amused by Craig, and from time to time she regarded him with smiling, ironical eyes. Once she lifted the olive from his martini and playfully dropped it into his mouth. Farris had difficulty understanding her game. She was no dumb little stenographer out to lunch with the boss. Or was this some elaborate parody of just such a person? He decided he liked her better. As he watched her, he now remembered the name. He had seen her by-line in the entertainment section of one of the weekend papers. Among other things, she interviewed visiting film actors and nightclub singers. He had also seen a piece or two by her in a column called "Life-styles."

The waiter brought several steaming dishes to their table and Farris took the opportunity to order another double scotch. Craig wagged a finger at him. "Charlie, eat some food. You're a walking shadow. For Christ sakes." He heaped vegetables and rice on Madeline Greene's plate. "Food and sex," he said. "You shouldn't neglect them." He was joking, but Farris sensed that Craig was sizing him up, for the man was shrewd and he hadn't survived in the magazine business for twenty years without understanding people. Now he was probably turning over in his mind the question of whether Charlie Farris was worth the risk of several hundred dollars. Or would he hole up somewhere and drink money like that away?

As they ate their lunch, Farris watched a couple at a nearby table. The woman, once beautiful, was in her early forties and still looked good, an aging Simone Signoret watching her weight by sipping Perrier water. Opposite her, toying with a beer, was a perfectly groomed man in his twenties. Under the table their hands were touching. At once Farris thought of Pat and Peter Neville, and of how everything seemed turned around. The young man with the blow-dried hair should have been eating with Madeline Greene, while Simone Signoret should have teamed up with Craig. And where did that leave Charlie Farris? He wasn't sure, and in any case he had to pay better attention because Craig was talking about this new job.

"So I was thinking the other night, Charlie. A first-rate writer like you ought to get back to work. You've been a little rusty lately. We haven't had anything from you for months now. I'll bet you it's almost a year. And now with this terrible tragedy. I'll be frank, Charlie, you could fall into trouble. I can see you sitting around and hitting the bottle. And believe me, that remark is not meant to embarrass you. That's spoken as a friend."

Madeline Greene lit a cigarette, striking the match hard. She looked mildly annoyed. Farris wondered if she was upset by Craig's rudeness. The editor lit a cigar. "So I talked it over the other night with Harry Menard, and we both agreed that we had to get Charlie Farris working again. The best tonic is hard work. What was it that Dr. Johnson said about sorrow or sadness?"

"Grief is a species of idleness," said Farris.

"That's it. Grief is a species of idleness."

"Is that Samuel Johnson?" asked Madeline Greene.

"The same," said Craig.

She wrinkled her nose. "I took a course in him at the university. What an old bore!"

"He was a great man," said Farris. For a moment they stared with dislike at each other. Craig regarded the tip of his olive-colored cigar. "Anyway, Charlie, the idea is a simple one. There's a helluva lot of interest in hockey down in the southeastern states. Places like Charleston and Richmond. That Southern League just packs them in, six, seven thousand every game. I want you to go down there and find out why. What is it that those crackers like about our rugged Canadian pastime? Probably it's the fighting. I think they see it as a kind of roller ball on ice. Anyway, you can stay a week, maybe ten days. We'll cover expenses and pay you the usual for a couple of thousand words. But I want you to interview the fans, the players, the coaches, the guy who sells beer in the arena. Get to know the players. Some of them are just fresh from little hick towns in northern Ontario and Saskatchewan, leather-jacketed young punks on the glory trail. Others must be old-timers with nowhere to go but down. Work some human interest into that." The girl was paying attention to all this. Through the cigar smoke Craig squinted at the luncheon bill and opened a billfold laden with credit cards.

"I'm not going to send down a photographer; you can get some location shots from the local papers. If not, we can get some file stuff. I don't see that as a problem. And here's another angle you might like to work in, Charlie. Some of those kids really like playing down there and now and then they get hooked up with a local belle. So you might interview some guy as father and husband. See how his lifestyle differs from ours, et cetera, et cetera. I think all this would make a damn good story. The hockey season is starting to move now. We could run this in early December." He turned to Madeline Greene. "You can't go wrong with a hockey story this time of year. Every time we feature a hockey story, we can expect a 10 percent rise in circulation. The other thing about this, Charlie, is what I said before. It will get you out of town for a while and maybe help you forget this terrible thing that's happened to you." Farris observed that it was like Craig to remind everyone of his charity and goodwill.

Farris rattled the ice cubes in his glass. "When would you like me to go?"

"As soon as possible," said Craig. "Why not go tomorrow or Sunday? You could be down there and ready to go by the first of the week. Book a flight this afternoon . . . pick your city. And when you get down there, rent a car. I talked to Menard about this and he says there are four games scheduled over the next week, all within a hundred and fifty miles of each other. You could take in a couple of those."

"What about an advance?" asked Farris. There it was, the old embarrassing question. In the writing business you were always asking someone for money. Farris often envied people who had salaries. But Craig took an evelope from his jacket. "There's a check for five. Okay?"

Later the three of them walked west against a sharp wind that watered Farris's weak eye. In the middle Craig held on to each of them like a friendly giant. As they leaned into the wind Madeline Greene muttered, "Goddamn winter is here already." Above them, Craig's voice boomed in the gray air: "Mady, if you're going to live in the true north, strong and freezing, you've got to learn to live with winter. Why don't you get yourself a pair of skis and take some lessons? You have to live with old man winter or he'll bury you. I myself can hardly wait until the skiing starts."

"It's not my thing," said Madeline. "I'm a city girl. I was always lousy at sports, too. Strapping two boards on your feet and schlepping through the snow is not my idea of a big time."

"It's good exercise," said Craig buoyantly. "And you could use some exercise, little princess. You're getting chubby."

"Yeh?" she said. "Well, that's my problem, isn't it?" She sounded resentful, though Craig laughed.

At the entrance to the parking lot Craig looked down at them. "Well, what about you, Mady? Are you coming back to the office? I'm tied up in a meeting in ten minutes." The girl's face was now reddened by the wind. "Jesus, it's cold. No, I want to go to the library, Ian, and look up some stuff. And, plus I have to go to the bank. Maybe Charlie here will give me a lift."

"Good idea," said Craig. "Charlie? You look like a frozen turd standing there. Give her a lift."

"Sure." He wiped his eye with a handkerchief. Craig laid a gloved hand on Farris's arm. "Listen, Charlie. Your friends feel deeply about what happened. Look . . . I feel deeply. I have two daughters, you know." Farris saw the man clearly through only one eye. He wanted desperately to get out of this bitter wind. "Do me a favor, will you, Charlie?" asked Craig.

"If I can."

"Don't spend all that money on booze. It can get

to you. I've heard stories. We all know you've had a rough year, but be careful. Okay?"

A rough year. He had lost a wife and son. "Rough year" was one way of putting it. The girl had turned her back to them and the wind. "You'll pull out of all this sooner or later," continued Craig. "Take care now and call me collect around the middle of next week. Let me know how things are going." He jabbed Madeline's back with a finger. "Hey, princess . . . remember now. We're going to do that layout on Sunday afternoon at three. Okay?"

"Right," she said, turning to them.

"Okay," said Craig. "Ciao, everyone." They watched him jog toward University Avenue, one hand holding on to his deerstalker.

"Let's go," said Madeline. "I'm freezing."

On the upper level of the parking lot they walked through the stink of cold motor exhaust and reached his Volkswagen. Once inside, Madeline shivered deep within her coat. "Jesus. It's good to be out of that wind." Farris gunned the motor, and soon warm air was blowing across their legs. He moved the little car down the ramp and, after paying the attendant, drove onto the street. Along the way he asked her how she liked working for Craig. Madeline shrugged. "Ian can be fun. He's a lot of fun to work with, but in many important ways he's an asshole."

Farris smiled. Many intelligent women talked like this nowadays, but it took some getting used to.

"In what important ways is he an asshole?" asked Farris. She glanced over at him with a look of impatience. "Oh, come on, Charlie. You're not stupid. You know Ian. He's pathetic. Maybe I shouldn't say that to you. You're probably a good friend of his."

"I've known him for a long time."

"How long?"

"Twelve . . . fifteen years."

"Well, you know him. . . God, he's so juvenile, so old-fashioned about certain things. He can publish a really enlightened article on, say, women and their place in today's world. But he himself remains a funny old thing out of the fifties, a horny old square who still carries a condom in his wallet." For the first time that week Farris laughed, a sharp bark of pleasure. Madeline grinned. "He thinks he's doing you a big favor if he lays you."

Still smiling, Farris asked her, "So why bother?" He thought he knew the answer.

Madeline shrugged again. "I need him right now. He's just given me this fantastic assignment. Two whole weeks in New York, expenses paid. Am I going to have a ball in that town!"

They were stopped by traffic at Bay and Dundas, and around them people hurried with heads tucked into coat collars. Others stepped forward like prisoners with both gloved hands covering their ears. Suddenly Madeline said, "Well, the hell with Ian anyway. Fiif."

"What?" asked Farris.

"Fiif," she said, half-turning toward him. "Meaning, fuck it, it's Friday. Why don't you let me buy you a drink, Charlie? I tell you what . . . I'll take you over to the club for a drink." She imitated a snooty Englishwoman and they both laughed. Then she said, "I'm serious, though. Do you want to go for a drink?"

Farris lit a cigarette. "Would your club be 21 McGill?"

"Yeh. Why?"

The little car bucked through the intersection and

Farris said, "I don't like the place very much, that's all."

"Now why is that, Charlie? You're being difficult. Do you know that?"

"Well, I met my wife there a few times. It was during the time we were deciding to break up our home." He remembered sitting with Pat in the handsome lounge. But it wasn't a good place for them to talk. Distracting female musk seemed to hang in the air. He had difficulty concentrating.

"I don't think I know your wife. What does she look like? No . . . don't tell me, I don't want to know. Who cares about your wife anyway? Hey—I've got a terrific idea. Why don't we go to your place? We could go to mine, but you won't believe this, I live out in High Park. I'm moving downtown at the end of the month. What do you say? You don't live far from here, do you? Ian said you were in Cabbagetown or something."

"I don't have anything to drink at home," Farris said.

Madeline frowned at him. "You don't exactly make a girl feel welcome, do you? Look, Charlie . . . I can get ten men to have a drink with me inside ten minutes, so if this is a great bore for you, just fucking say so and you can drop me off here at Yonge." They were now at the corner of Yonge and Dundas where, in another few hours, he would meet Donald Howard and talk about Jonathan's murder. Thinking about it excited him. "I could use a drink," he said. "I'll pick some up." They stopped at a liquor store and he bought several bottles of whiskey and, for a change, some rum. By the time he returned to the car, the girl had recovered her good humor. As he placed the heavy bag on the rear floor she laughed. "Jesus, what are you having, the neighborhood over?"

"I'm thirsty," replied Farris lamely.

On their way into the Del Monte Arms she took his arm. "You know, I'll be glad to move closer into town. You're right down where the action is, aren't you?" He looked at her severely as he opened the door. "Yes," he said. "Right downtown where the action is, as you put it." She remembered then. "I'm sorry, Charlie. I didn't mean it like that." In the lobby Mrs. Farnsworth stood waiting for the elevator in her new plum-colored coat. When she saw them, she flushed and looked upward at the floor numbers above the elevator door.

"Good afternoon, Mrs. Farnsworth," said Farris.

"Good afternoon, Mr. Farris," she said without looking at him. The elevator door opened and Farris stepped in behind the two women. As they rose in silence, Farris was distressed by the thought that within a week of his son's death he was again bringing a strange woman to his apartment. Why he should see anything wicked in that he couldn't really say, yet it seemed somehow wrong. He felt bad, too, about Mrs. Farnsworth and their grotesque evening together. Watching her fit the key into her door lock, he was filled with a vague sadness. He wanted to tell her that he was sorry, though about what he couldn't say.

In his apartment he made drinks while Madeline watched. "Easy on mine, Charlie," she warned. "I don't drink much." She walked around his living room. "Your place is nice and neat. You must have someone come in."

Farris handed her a drink. "No, I do it myself. I'm an old veteran of the vacuum cleaner."

Madeline sipped her drink. "Jesus, I can't stand

any of that stuff. I'm a real slob and I admit it. If I had my way, I'd live in hotels. I love hotels. When I was a kid, we'd go to Florida for a couple of weeks every March. And we always stayed at a hotel in Miami Beach, and that was it for me. People made your bed, did your laundry, served your breakfast. I guess I'm just physically lazy. In school I was a real zero when it came to dopey things like gym class. I can still hear Miss Hawkins, our gym teacher, yelling, 'Greenberg, try those parallel bars again. Put some effort into it.' Ha. . ."

"Why did you change your name?" asked Farris.

"What?" She looked surprised. "Oh, you mean from Greenberg to Greene? With an *e*, by the way. Oh, I don't know. I once went with this guy named Myron Schacter and he was training to be a dentist and he was going to make a lot of money, which by the way he has. Anyway, Myron had this theory about names. He said it was important for people to remember your name. It was good for business, more professional. I don't know if it helped Myron make his pile, but anyway, when I got my first job on the *Star*, I changed it to Greene. That's with an *e*, by the way. Why do you ask?"

"I don't know," said Farris. "I guess I don't think a person should change his name. It's something to do with family, but don't ask me to explain it. It's hard to put into words."

They drank in silence while she inspected his record collection. Then she turned to him and said, "Hey, I read your novel a couple of nights ago. It was really good." He looked at her uneasily, still surprised when he met someone who had read his book. "I mean it," she said, "It was really good. Why didn't you ever write another one?"

"Some things got in the way," he said. "I started a couple of others, but somehow they didn't work out. And then . . ." He paused and added, "Some people have only one book in them. I think I'm one of those people." Admitting it was not easy, but he was glad he had said it. "Why would you want to read my novel?" he asked.

"No particular reason," she said. "A few days ago Ian told me we'd be having lunch with you, so I just wanted to know what kind of a book you'd written. I've not read any of your magazine pieces. I hate jock stuff. I went with a football player in university for a while. That was enough for me."

Farris was again thinking of his son's murder and of the strange telephone call. After a moment he lifted his head to find her smiling at him.

"Half a dollar for your thoughts, Charlie. . . Inflation, you know."

He smiled. "I'm sorry. I've just got some things on my mind."

She put aside her unfinished drink, and placed her arms around his neck. "That's all right. Don't worry about it." She looked up at him, half-grinning. "Let's fuck. It's good for tension. And you're tense, baby. Your shoulder muscles are all tight." She was kneading his shoulders. Farris put his arms around her. "What is this 'Let's fuck'? The new mating call?"

Her long fingers stroked the back of his neck. "Now, don't come on like an old fogy, Charlie. You know you'd like to fuck me. I'm a damned attractive woman. Someday I'll be old and fat and wrinkled. Right now I'm a big lush peach, and you know it."

"You are beautiful," he said as they kissed.

And in the bedroom how quickly she shucked off her clothes and prepared for him. Young people nowadays were so sure of themselves in sex, thought Farris as he watched her. When he was this girl's age, he was still overwhelmed by the mystery of it all. There was something exotic and furtive about such passion. It was as if in those times he couldn't believe that such happiness was available to ordinary people. In bed he had read passages by Henry Miller and D.H. Lawrence to his first wife. But Darlene said they were dirty and she didn't want to hear them. And so under cover of darkness they had made quick, violent love over and over again. But here in the afternoon light in another age it was different. And for a time, Farris forgot his troubles and thanked creation for this splendid loving creature beside him. When he came inside her, he looked down at her grieving face.

"I'm very slow, Charlie, don't take offense. I'm nearly there."

Slowly, then, he kissed her throat and breasts while with eyes closed and open-mouthed she fulfilled herself, rising finally with a cry to her moment. When it was over, she lay panting beside him. With his hand on her breast he could feel her pounding heart. "That was nice, Charlie. You're a patient man. Some guys don't like me doing that. Their sense of manhood or something gets all flustered."

"Save the flattery," he said, lying back. "I don't need it." She rose on one elbow to stare at him outraged. "Hey, I'm not flattering anybody. I said that was nice and I fucking well meant it. Don't accuse me of being any bullshit artist. I don't like that at all." She had turned her back to him now, and was curled up like a little sulky teenager. Farris stared thoughtfully at her broad, rounded back and bum. How vulnerable a naked woman looks, he thought. Is this what the Viking or the Goth saw when he drew aside the hut's curtain? His mind teemed with brutal imagery, and he put his arms around her to protect her. "Don't be angry with me," he said.

"You're such a touchy bastard," she said to the wall.

"That's true," he said, "I am touchy."

She turned heavy-breasted toward him. He could see she wasn't one to bear a grudge. "I'm sorry about your son, Charlie. You've probably heard that from all kinds of people, but I really am sorry. I don't have a kid and I don't ever want to have one. Well, maybe that's bullshit, but I don't think so." She touched his face and smiled. "I'm sorry, that's all." Farris kissed her hand. This was a loving girl and, behind the swagger, a kind one. He swung his legs over the side of the bed. "I'm going to get another drink." Madeline reached for her handbag, calling after him, "You drink too much. And don't think I'm nagging. But, shit . . . I guess I am. Twenty-three and already I sound like my mother."

When he returned, she was sitting up in bed smoking a joint. The smoke hung over the room and sweetened the stale air. "I don't suppose you want one of these, Charlie?" she asked.

"No thanks."

She settled back against a pillow while Farris thought again about the caller. He must soon get organized; he must get the money and the airline ticket. He lay thinking about all this, considering whether he should try to reach Grahame. That was surely the sensible thing to do. Grahame could follow them to the airport and, once there, arrest this Donald Howard, whoever he was. And if he was just a crazy on the loose, they could put him away as a common nuisance. If, on the other hand, he did know something about the murder, the cops could get it out of him. Yet something within Farris resisted the idea of telling Grahame just yet. Beside him Madeline said, "I wish I could go down South with you, Charlie. I hate hockey, but it would be fun going along with you. All those crummy motel strips outside of small towns. The little bars with Schlitz signs on the windows. Lousy meals at Howard Johnson's. Eating Big Macs on the road. It would be a great experience."

Experience! It was one of her favorite words, he thought. She gathered experiences the way a squirrel gathered acorns for the winter. Not a bad way of looking at things, perhaps.

"When are you leaving anyway?" she asked.

"I don't know. I had a telephone call this morning. It upset me."

He didn't know why he had mentioned it, and immediately he regretted doing so. The cannabis smoke irritated his failing eye.

"Was it about your son?" she asked.

"Yes."

"A crank call?"

"I don't know yet." He was afraid to continue; he had already said too much, and impatiently he heaved himself up and got out of bed.

"I've got things to do."

"Well, okay, okay, take it easy." She stubbed out her joint.

"I can take a hint, for Christ sakes." She leaned across the bed, searching for her clothes. Looking down at her, Farris said, "I'm sorry. There's just something I have to do." She sat now on the edge of the bed working on a pair of beige pantyhose. "Do you want to tell me about this phone call, Charlie?"

"No," he said flatly.

"Thanks a lot for trusting me, baby," she said, as she stood up snapping the long stockings' waistband. Beside her, Farris pulled on his pants and said nothing.

CHAPTER THREE

Yonge Street between Queen and Carlton used to be called the Strip. Once notorious for massage parlors and bawdy houses, which the cops had closed down, the street still had a kind of seedy glamour for sightseers. The east side was lined with taverns and strip shows, movie houses and fast-food places. From record shops and disco joints, rock music spilled across the sidewalk, crowded at all hours by young people and tourists from Buffalo and Detroit.

At ten minutes to seven Farris wheeled his little car north from King, maneuvering into the curb lane. The department stores were open for Christmas business, and Friday-night traffic clogged the street in both directions. Sober and nervous, Farris lit another cigarette and inched the Volkswagen forward. In the inside pocket of his jacket was a one-way ticket to Vancouver endorsed in the name of Donald Howard, and a thick envelope containing fifty twenty-dollar bills. Sitting in the dense traffic, Farris felt both foolish and apprehensive. He was sure now that he should have phoned Grahame and let him handle this. Meeting this guy on his own was like going to a quack to cure cancer. Feeling ashamed, he put the car in gear and moved forward another half a block. At

Shuter Street a drunk stood wavering in front of the Silver Rail Tavern, trying to hail a cab. The fellow was far gone, his overcoat open to his shirt and his tie removed. From time to time he lifted a tiny porkpie hat in homage to passing ladies. A Friday-night drunk!

Farris saw himself a few years ago when he, too, had emerged from a tavern after several hours of drinking with friends. He remembered the boozy good-byes and the sobering taxi ride home where Pat waited with her cold supper. Yet sometimes the force of his humor had been enough to coax her from ill temper, and sometimes, too, he had put on music and danced with his mildly protesting wife while his five-year-old son clapped his hands with happiness. Later he took them out for Chinese food. How he now craved for just such an ordinary evening as that!

Ahead of him was Dundas and Yonge, bright with neon. Yet, to his dismay, the traffic light turned green. He moved ahead slowly, but behind him a cab's horn blared. Cursing, Farris stayed where he was, convinced now that he was the victim of some monstrous hoax. Angrily the taxi driver pulled out, just missing another car, whose horn squawked in protest. As the cab sped past, the driver, a young bushy-haired man, yelled an obscenity at Farris and raised two fingers. In the rear seat the drunk lifted his ludicrous hat in greeting and the taxi shot through the intersection. Farris felt himself perspiring behind the ears. Here he was in front of the bookstore! Where was the bastard? Behind him another horn sounded, but then the passenger door opened, and a slight, pale young man in a soiled oversized trenchcoat jumped in and slammed the door.

Without looking at his passenger, Farris gunned the Beetle through the orange traffic light, while the youth coughed, a dry, rattling, unhealthy sound. He appeared to be wearing only an undershirt and jeans beneath the ill-fitting coat. Glancing down, Farris saw sockless feet in old white sneakers. Very tense, the young man kept looking behind them as Farris turned left on Elm Street and passed the Balkan Restaurant where he and Pat had once held hands in the candlelight. And here he was passing that old romantic haunt on what he now considered to be some kind of outlandish misadventure. On this quiet street the young man spoke at last in a light, nervous voice. "You were right on time, Mr. Farris."

"I don't like to keep people waiting," said Farris inanely. He now looked sideways at Donald Howard. Farris guessed the youth was no more than twenty or so, sickly looking and lost in his vast coat. His rather delicate face was ravaged and thin to the point of emaciation. Too young to be a wino; he was most probably a junkie, thought the writer. The boy gave off a bad odor.

At Bay Street, Farris waited for the traffic to clear. "All right," he said. "I take it that you are the person I spoke to on the telephone this morning. So we're now on our way to the airport. I'll go over to Avenue Road and then up to 401. I've got your money and your ticket, so that's my side of the deal. Right?" The young man said nothing. He appeared to be trembling, though whether from cold or nerves Farris couldn't tell. But Farris was again seized by the notion that he was the victim of some enormous practical joke in appalling taste. Possibly it was the handiwork of a madman. He suspected that at this very moment the people who had sent the boy on this crazy errand were beside themselves with laughter. And all at Farris's expense. He glanced quickly in the rearview mirror, and near the Hospital for Sick Children he pulled over to the curb. Reaching up, he switched on the interior light and turned to face the young man. "All right, let's have a good look at you," he said. In the light the boy looked frail indeed. Farris flicked off the light and then, reaching over, pulled the young man toward him. Farris's voice was thick with anger. "All right, you. I've seen your face and now I want to know what the fuck is going on. Is this some joke or what? I'm not driving all the way out to that fucking airport without hearing what you've got to say."

Two nurses walked past and looked back as they made their way toward the hospital. Mindful of the absurdity of his situation, Farris again shook the youth, who offered no resistance. "Come on, goddamn it. What's all this about?"

"Please, Mr. Farris," said the young man. "Let go of me. You're hurting me." Farris tightened his grip, feeling strangely powerful but also ashamed. Would he do this if the young man were healthy and stronger? This boy was cowardly and weak as a kitten. Yet it felt good to be punishing someone. He had endured a terrible week of frustration and rage and now he was punishing someone for it. Was this how the cops felt after looking for suspects for weeks on end? He didn't know. All Farris knew was that it felt good to have purchase on this young man's coat. And further, he knew he would very much enjoy driving his fist into this pale, frightened face. Yet all this was attended by an unyielding shame.

Finally he released the young man, pushing him back against the door. "All right. Give me the story or I'm going to pull you out of this car and kick the shit out of you right on the sidewalk. Then I'm going to drive to the nearest cop station and have them book you as a common fucking nuisance. Or worse.

And you better believe they'll kick you around a helluva lot harder than I ever could. They don't like people who are tied up with killers of children. Then, in the cells, you'll find that most of the prisoners won't take too kindly to you either."

"I didn't kill anybody," the young man cried. It was very nearly a wail filled with misery and hopelessness. There were tears in his eyes. But Farris was not about to relent. "But you know someone who did. Right? How would you like me to drive right now to the nearest cop station and have them ask you some questions?" In fact, he was half-thinking of doing just that. But it seemed to be the thing that most terrified the youth. "You didn't tell them, did you?" he asked desperately. "You promised, Mr. Farris. You said you'd give me eight hours. You gave me your word." The boy's whining enraged Farris, and he struck him across the face with an open hand.

"I don't have to give you fuck all," said Farris. "You better start telling me something." The youth was now openly weeping.

"Please don't hit me. I didn't kill your little boy. Please take me to the airport. You promised." Farris briefly wondered if his passenger was on drugs. But now he could also see that the two nurses had stopped and were looking back at them. It occurred to Farris that what was going on inside his car must look very fishy to strangers. He reached across and locked the passenger door. "All right," he said slowly as they pulled away. "Let's have it. We'll go for our drive and you can talk to me. For a start, who are you and what do you know about my son's death?"

The young man had stopped crying and was now sniffling back tears like a child. In his lap his thin, reddened hands twisted a Kleenex.

"My name is Donald Stewart, not Howard. I come

from a small town up north. I came to Toronto two years ago last summer. I just quit school and came here because I couldn't stand that town anymore. So I came to Toronto and met Marty."

"Look," interrupted Farris, "I don't want your fucking life history, all right? Now, Marty who? What's his name? And what's he got to do with my son?" Donald Stewart looked distraught.

"I'm trying to tell you that, Mr. Farris. If you'll only give me a chance."

"All right. So you met this Marty." Farris could now see that in fundamental ways the young man was still a child, and he would insist on telling his story his way. "Marty's mother," said Donald, "ran a rooming house and I went there one day looking for a room and Marty came to the door and I just knew I'd be happy there. And I was, too. For nearly a year. You see, Marty and me were lovers. He's the most wonderful, sweet person." The tears had started again. They were now passing the dark Victorian bulk of the Provincial Legislature as they traveled north toward Bloor Street. As Donald wiped his eyes, Farris wondered where this story was heading and how Johnny fit into all this. He would have to be patient. The boy seemed deeply frightened and what he appeared to need most was a listener.

At Bloor Street they stopped for a red light and Farris offered the youth a cigarette. But Donald shook his head; he didn't smoke tobacco. "Okay, Donald," said Farris. "So what happened after that?" The boy heaved a sigh.

"Everything was super. I got a job at Coca-Cola. It wasn't much of a job really, but I didn't care. Marty and I had great times together. I mean we really loved one another. Marty doesn't make that many friends. You see, he's a little slow. I don't mean he's simple or anything, but he's never had much of a chance. His mother is so protective. I mean she will hardly let him leave the house by himself and he's nearly twenty-five. He's almost a prisoner. So at first she was glad I was there because I was a kind of companion for him, you see. The only place she would take him was to the wrestling matches at the Gardens. She loves wrestling matches. And after a while I went along too, though both Marty and me found it all so boring. All those repulsive fat men. Anyway, Mrs. Poole then found out that Marty and me were lovers. She caught us in bed one night and I thought she'd kill me. But instead she just seemed not to care. She never was very keen on me, but she didn't say anything. As long as Marty was happy. So everything was fine until last summer when Snapshot came to live in the house."

"Snapshot?" asked Farris. "Who is he, Donald?"

"He's a disgusting person, Mr. Farris. A horrible man."

Farris felt curiously affected. Snapshot! Marty! Hadn't Jonathan's diary mentioned two characters labeled S. and M.? Farris no longer believed he was being duped.

"Snapshot came to rent a room," said Donald. "And in a few days he had Mrs. Poole and Marty eating out of his hands. Oh, I won't deny that he can be funny and he can be a very friendly person if he wants something from you. He can be likable if you don't see through him. Anyway, Marty and his mother thought he was super. He was always bringing beer and pizza back to the house for them. He always seemed to have plenty of money, though he never worked at anything. He used to belong to this motorcycle gang and some of his friends would drop by the house. They were real toughs. Anyway, Snapshot was soon taking Marty and his mother to the wrestling matches and to the movies and stock-car races and things like that. I wasn't invited anymore. It was just like I was shut out of their lives. And then one night I heard Snapshot sneaking into Mrs. Poole's room. And the sounds that came from there. Well, Snapshot's about thirty, you see, and Mrs. Poole must be fifty or sixty. I guess she was grateful for anything. Anyway, after that Snapshot could do absolutely nothing wrong and I thought to myself, great . . . he can have her, just leave Marty and me alone. And then . . ." The tears had started again and Farris warned himself not to be impatient.

"Take your time, Donald. What happened then?"

"Then one night, a few weeks after Snapshot moved in, I found them together in bed."

Farris said nothing.

"She wasn't enough for him, you see. He had to have Marty too, the bastard."

Farris kept his counsel. He was listening to a spurned lover, and such a person always made an excellent informer. Northbound traffic on Avenue Road was heavy, and Farris drove with care. He wanted no minor accidents to interfere with Donald's story. In a way, he was glad now that Grahame had been out when he telephoned. "So, Donald . . . this Snapshot character sort of took over the household. Is that it? Were there other tenants?"

"Oh yes. It was a big rooming house and Mrs. Poole has made a lot of money out of it over the years. She's now sold the place to a developer. It's on Ontario Street and all the smarties are moving in there now. She got a lot of money for it. She has to be out by the end of the year. And that's what I think Snapshot is interested in, her money. There is no Mr. Poole, by the way. He was kicked out when Marty was a baby. Marty doesn't remember him. But Snapshot did all sorts of jobs around the house. And he bullied other people. Told us to make sure our rooms were clean and not to play our radios too loud. A couple of people moved out because he was so bossy. He thought he was the king of the castle and just because he was balling that old bitch. Most of the time, though, he sat in his room fiddling with his cameras."

"His cameras?" Farris asked with a quickening heartbeat. Grahame had mentioned pictures.

"Yes. He and Marty would spend hours looking at pictures and sometimes taking them. He would give Marty a joint and then take his picture naked. Snapshot had hundreds of pictures of naked boys. Some he took himself and others he bought from people. Then he'd sell them, you see, in beer parlors or restaurants. One day I told him to stop taking pictures of Marty. It didn't seem somehow right to be taking advantage of Marty like that. But he just laughed at me and called me filthy names. So I told Mrs. Poole everything. How Snapshot and Marty were lovers and how they smoked dope and took dirty pictures. She was furious with me and wouldn't believe a word I said. She said I was making it all up because I was just another jealous fairy. So I lost my temper. I have a temper when I'm angry. And I told her that her big lover boy was making a fool of her by sleeping with her son and feeding him dope and taking dirty pictures." The boy seemed to gain strength by telling his story.

"She nearly killed me, Mr. Farris. She's a big bitch and very strong. She twisted my arm until I cried and she knocked my head against the wall and threw me out of her kitchen. Then she told Snapshot and he came up to my room and started packing my clothes for me. Then he picked me up—actually picked me up and carried me down the stairs and out onto the street. It was the middle of the day and everyone was laughing at me. And Snapshot warned me, too. He said he'd kill me if I told anyone about him and Marty and the pictures."

"When did all this happen, Donald?"

"Just a couple of months ago. On Labour Day weekend."

"So you moved out and this Snapshot stayed on with Marty and his mother?"

"Yes. I didn't move far. You see, I'm still in love with Marty in a way and I think he still loves me. He's scared of Snapshot now. So I moved a few blocks away and I used to see Marty and Snapshot walking around Allan Gardens. That's where Snapshot sometimes sold his dope and pictures."

Farris felt suddenly sour in the stomach. He believed now that he was about to hear something enormously vile. His throat seemed congested as he asked softly, "And where did Johnny fit into all this, Donald?"

The boy hesitated. "Well, as I said before, I used to watch Snapshot and Marty in the park, and now and then they would be alone or maybe just have a young kid with them. I even phoned Marty once and said, 'Look, Marty, stay away from kids because that's bad.' But he only laughed and said there was no harm. They were just having a little fun. Sometimes they'd take one of these kids back to Mrs. Poole's and give him money."

They were now mounting the ramp to the westbound 401 and Farris accelerated to keep pace with the fast-moving freeway traffic. A huge tractor-trailer thundered past them and in its wake the Volkswagen shuddered. Donald Stewart was once again listless as he talked. "I saw your son with Snapshot and Marty a couple of times, Mr. Farris," he said quietly. "It was always on a Saturday. I think he was buying grass from them." It was painful to hear, but it fit perfectly with Grahame's suspicions. Farris whispered his question. His throat and chest seemed too full. "Did Snapshot kill him, Donald?"

"I'm still holding you to your promise, Mr. Farris. I'm sticking my neck out here."

"Just answer the fucking question, Donald . . . please."

"Last Monday night Marty phoned me and asked if he could come over. He sounded really scared. He said he was being treated like a prisoner. His mother wouldn't let him out of her sight, but he said he had to see me. He was going to sneak out when she was sleeping. Snapshot had gone up to the farm on Sunday, but Mrs. Poole wouldn't let Marty go. So he sneaked out and came to see me late Monday night and he told me everything. He was nearly hysterical, Mr. Farris, and said he just had to tell someone. He didn't know what to do or where to go. He told me how Snapshot met your son last Saturday afternoon in Allan Gardens. And then Snapshot suggested that your son go back with him to Mrs. Poole's. So he brought the boy back to his room and Marty was there and they all smoked some grass. It was powerful stuff." The boy now looked out his window as he spoke. "Then after a while Snapshot thought it would be fun to take some pictures and he offered your son some money. . ." He stopped and Farris said thickly, "Go on with it."

"Well, Marty says that Snapshot then suggested they have sex with the boy. At first the boy thought it was just fooling around, but then things got out of control. They were very high, Mr. Farris. Marty doesn't even remember some of it very clearly."

Farris could already hear the man saying that in court.

"Marty didn't kill him, Mr. Farris. Snapshot did. The boy didn't like what was happening, and I guess he started to make a noise." Now Donald was again crying. "It's so awful."

Above the whine of the motor Farris heard himself screaming, "You think it was awful, do you? What do you think it was like for my son? Snapshot was giving it to him up the ass and the boy was screaming in pain, so they put a pillow over his head to stop him from making all that noise. Oh, Jesus . . . Jesus . . . Jesus . . . Jesus . . . Jesus." The car was shimmying badly, and, looking down through blurred eyes, Farris saw that in anger he had pressed the little car to beyond eighty miles an hour. Breathing through his mouth like a runner, he slowly eased back the accelerator and swung in behind a truck.

"Is that what happened, Donald?" he asked.

"Yes."

"Then when he was dead, they stuffed him in garbage bags and threw him behind a factory, right? How did they do that, Donald? Tell me about it."

Farris was calmer now. He knew at last what had happened and he seemed to hear his own heart ticking over lightly and strongly like a small motor. He reminded himself to drive carefully. There must be no accidents, though danger and death seemed constant and pervasive. In the glare of passing lights Donald's thin face shone palely. "Marty told his mother what they had done," said Donald. "Snapshot didn't want to, but they were confused. It had all happened so quickly. And so when Marty realized what they had done, he told his mother. He was in a panic, you see. But Mrs. Poole made him go to sleep. She gave him sleeping pills, and then Snapshot and her took your son away. They used Mrs. Poole's truck."

Farris lit another cigarette and opened the window to admit the cold air. "Okay, Donald. You've told me the story. Now, where are these people?"

"They've gone up to the farm," Donald said. "It's an old farm that Mrs. Poole bought a couple of years ago. Sometimes she rents it out to friends of Snapshot's, bikers. Marty and his mother went up on Tuesday. She got this guy Earl to look after her place because there's nobody living there now, you see. This Earl is another biker friend of Snapshot's. Earl earns his living peddling speed and beating up people. He'll break your arm for a couple of hundred dollars. I bought some speed from him last summer, but I'd never go back to him again. He cheated me and there wasn't a thing I could do about it. Anyway, this Earl is looking after the house while Marty and his mother and Snapshot are staying up at the farm until things settle down, I guess. But you see, Mrs. Poole found out somehow that Marty had visited me last Monday night and told me everything. Anyway, she phoned me yesterday and asked me to come up to the farm for the weekend. I was up there a couple of times last summer. But yesterday Mrs. Poole said that Marty missed me and why didn't I go and spend a few days with him and then maybe Marty and I could go away for a holiday. Maybe down to Florida or someplace like that for a few weeks. She said Marty was lonely and needed a companion. But see, I don't trust her, Mr. Farris. There is no way I'm going up there. So I told her that I don't have any money, which is the truth, and she said don't worry about that. Just go over to the house and speak to Earl and he would give me enough money to catch the bus and then they would meet me at the bus terminal at Poulton. But I said I wasn't going to do that and she got really nasty and said I had better get up there and I also better keep my mouth shut if I knew what was good for me. So I said keep my mouth shut about what. And she said, 'Don't be a goddamn little smart aleck, Donald. Just keep your mouth shut and get up here.' "

Farris listened intently as he drove. To the south the lights of the city flowed past them. "Does this Earl know anything about Johnny's murder?" asked Farris.

"I don't think so. I think just the four of us and you know what happened. All Earl knows is that Snapshot and Mrs. Poole want me up at the farm, and if they want me, Earl will get me. Unless I can get away from here. Late last night Earl came around to my room with a couple of friends. Lucky for me I was in the hall toilet and I came around the corner and there they were at my door. But their backs were to me and they didn't see me, so I ducked underneath the stairs. But they just stood there knocking on my door for the longest time. Then they went in my room and looked around. I was so scared I didn't even go back to my room. I took this coat from a neighbor's room. I had to wear something. It was freezing outside. But I've been frightened all day. I've spent the whole day in movie houses. I had ten dollars, but that's all gone now, so you can see why I have to get away from here."

"Okay," said Farris. "I understand that. But you know you're in serious trouble, don't you? I mean, you're an accessory after the fact, Donald. You can go to jail for that. You've known about a murder since last Monday night and you haven't gone to the police."

"I was too scared, Mr. Farris. I'm scared of the police. I'm afraid they'd involve me, see . . . I've been in trouble before."

"What kind of trouble?"

The boy looked out his window again. "I was acquitted. They never proved anything. It was such a silly charge. They raided a house I was in. We were minding our own business."

"What was the charge, Donald?"

The youth said it quickly. "Gross indecency."

Along Airport Road the motels blazed with light and Farris thought he would have enjoyed a couple of drinks in one of those crowded bars. Yet he drove on toward the airport. Donald Stewart turned to him.

"But Marty's mother said such awful things to me. She threatened to have Snapshot and Marty swear that I was with them last Saturday. She said they would involve me."

"But if you weren't there, you can prove it, can't you?" Donald seemed to shrivel within his coat. "That's just it, I can't prove anything. I drank a bottle of lemon gin by myself last Saturday night in my room. And I fell asleep. But look at it this way. I was probably seen around Allan Gardens Saturday afternoon. I have been known to go to certain kinds of parties. I know Snapshot and Marty. Who's going to believe me? It's so hopeless, see. . . They could pin anything on me."

He stopped and turned again to the window. "That's why I decided to call you, Mr. Farris. I told myself I'd take a chance. I'd tell you everything and hope you'd believe me. I'm so sick of all this. I haven't slept all week. Right now I just want to get out of Toronto."

Looking over at him, Farris could see how ill and frightened the boy was.

By luck there was an empty space at the metered parking lot near Departures, and Farris maneuvered the VW into the space and killed the engine. "All right, Donald. Where's this rooming house and where's this farm you've been talking about?" The young man stared at the floor, looking utterly spent. "You will give me a few hours, won't you, Mr. Farris?"

"Be nice now, Donald, and tell me where these people are."

Stewart told him the address of the rooming house on Ontario Street. It was only a few blocks from the Del Monte Arms. The farm was near a town called Poulton about a hundred and fifty miles northeast of Toronto. Farris knew the place. He made the boy repeat the directions several times, but he never wavered in his description. Farris also asked him to describe Snapshot and Marty and Mrs. Poole. Around them people were hurrying to catch planes, and for an instant Farris envied the travelers. He wouldn't have minded a plane ride right now. Aboard he could have a few drinks and something to eat. Wake up hours later in mild, rainy Vancouver. Behind the glass doors to the departure lounge he saw two Mounties talking to one another.

Farris handed the ticket and the envelope of money to Donald Stewart. "Have a good trip, Donald."

The youth closed his eyes and said, "Thank God you believed me." He got out of the car and, standing by the door, looked in at Farris. "They're up there, Mr. Farris. Snapshot is the one who did it. Marty needs help. He needs doctors to help him. He's really a very fine person. He didn't mean for any of this to happen. I'm sorry about your little boy. Marty said he was a nice kid." And then he was gone, trotting toward the glass doors, awkward and ludicrous in the dirty trenchcoat. Farris smoked and watched him go, gravely conscious of the possibility that he might just have committed a major folly in his life.

CHAPTER FOUR

Upon awakening Saturday morning, Farris hazily recalled a telephone conversation with Bill Langford the night before. It was late when Bill had called, though by then Farris had forgotten time. After returning from the airport, he had drunk most of a bottle of whiskey while thinking about Donald Stewart's story. He had also looked up the name Poole in the telephone directory, and there it was, an Emma Poole on Ontario Street.

When Bill called, he sounded drunk too, and he invited Farris to a requiem Mass for Jonathan on Saturday morning, to be followed by a family breakfast. Bill drunkenly insisted that Farris attend. Pat and Neville had not yet left for the Cayman Islands but were going on Sunday. This would be the last family breakfast together. Farris finally said he would go to the breakfast, though he didn't think he could make the mass. Although he didn't say so, he had endured enough of Bunny Buckley's services over the years. But Bill held Farris to his promise to attend breakfast, and now, sitting on the edge of his bed, he wished he had refused. Farris wasn't at all sure that he wanted to see Pat again. Moreover, he was now anxious to visit the farm. The night before, he had agonized over calling Grahame, knowing full well that it was the proper course to take. Yet he didn't, and sometime in the night he had decided to go to the farm himself, though just what he intended to do once he got there was unclear in his mind. All he knew was that he wanted to have a look at these people. And now he must get this damn breakfast out of the way.

These family breakfasts were an old Langford tradition, usually held after church on Sundays. Never having had much family life as a child, Farris used to enjoy them, recognizing in them the worth of formal habits. When Pat's mother was alive, the family had sat down to an elaborate meal. There was silver cutlery and starched linen napkins. Always a single glass of sherry was served beforehand. Farris remembered how, in the first few years of his marriage, he and Pat used to recover from Saturday-night parties by drinking cold beer in a little pantry off the kitchen. On one memorable Sunday Pat had raised her skirt and Farris, pressing her against the wall, had entered her not ten feet from the sound of family voices. On that occasion she laid a bite on his neck that he had to cover with his hand throughout the meal. But after Mrs. Langford's death the breakfasts changed. Instead of sherry, large Bloody Marys were served, and in the summer they left the dining room to sit in the garden on patio chairs, balancing omelettes on their knees. These breakfasts were once a part of the family's pattern of life, but now Farris doubted whether they had them more than a few times a year. Doubtless at Christmas and birthdays. And deaths! Farris knew he was no longer a member of the family, but he suspected that for sentimental reasons Bill wanted him there. During the call last night Bill had cried miserably and said how much he missed his grandson and Farris and where had his family and his happiness gone. And if this was what happened to a man at sixty-eight years of age, then Bill was no longer sure that he wanted to go on. At the end they were both in tears.

After Bill's call, Farris had drunkenly dialed several wrong numbers before reaching Madeline Greene's place. Unsure of what he wanted to say or do, he waited while a man answered. In the background Farris heard music and laughter, and the sounds enraged him. When Madeline came to the phone, she sounded high. And when she invited him over to the party, he thought he remembered yelling at her and calling her an insensitive bitch. Now, dressing slowly, Farris groaned at the memory. In fact he could not exactly recall what he had said to the girl, though he had the drunk's uncomfortable feeling that he had uttered base and unforgivable things. After he hung up on her, he broke his phonograph needle trying to play an old jazz record, and in anger hurled the record against the wall. In his sleep he dreamed he heard the phone ringing. Now, after drinking several cups of coffee, he felt strong enough to meet the day, and he stood by his window in shirt sleeves. Only a week ago he had stood here looking forward to his afternoon with Jonathan. Now he wondered how long such pain lasted. As he gazed down at the street, a taxi stopped in front of the building, and a moment later Mrs. Farnsworth came out of the lobby struggling with an immense suitcase. The driver got out to help her. It looked as though she was off to Portugal to see her husband, and Farris was glad for her, though when the taxi was out of sight he experienced an odd sense of loss. And minutes later, driving toward his father-in-law's house, he silently wished for his neighbor a safe journey.

When he passed the Langford house, it looked empty. But then it was not quite eleven, so he drove on to avoid waiting by their doorstep. Instead, he cruised the neighboring streets with their great brick houses and large trees. Along the sidewalks children, bundled up against the raw day, ran and played. And on the cold grass in front of their houses men raked leaves. To Farris it seemed his fate always to arrive early at the Langfords', and before he married Pat he had walked these streets time after time. Pat was notoriously unpunctual, and Farris had preferred to walk the streets rather than endure conversation with Mrs. Langford. So now, gray-faced and wearing dark glasses, Farris drove along several familiar streets, like a man hunting an address. He even passed Ian Craig's house and saw the editor in plaid jacket and toque putting on winter windows. Beside him his long, bony wife sprayed the panes with Windex. Today a family man, but tomorrow afternoon Craig would doubtless be draping Madeline Greene across his desk. Farris wished again that he hadn't telephoned the girl.

After rounding the block several times, he found a parking spot a block from the Langford house. And here he sat, feeling again that peculiar isolation which always accompanied him when he drew near the Langford house. In a few minutes they arrived in procession with Bill's heavy dark Chrysler leading the way, followed by Teddy's station wagon and Pat's Mercedes. The driveway was filled and Bunny Buckley had to park his Volvo on the street. Farris watched as the family filed into the house, with Bill and Teddy holding on to Lavinia Langford as she mounted the veranda steps. Teddy's two daughters raced across the lawn, and Farris watched with envy as Neville put an arm around Pat's shoulders and kissed her. Sylvia and Buckley followed them up the steps and into the house. Having watched them like this, Farris felt foolish and humiliated. He believed now that he should never have accepted Bill's invitation. He should not be wasting his time while Jonathan's killers were free. Yet he got out of the car and walked down the street to the house.

CHAPTER FIVE

For Farris the long, curving veranda of the Langford house was a place of good memories. Here in the evenings of early summer he and Bill Langford used to sit on old wicker chairs behind the vines of Dutchman's-pipe and sip Jack Daniel's. Each winter Bill and his wife went south for several weeks, to Florida and then to stay with cousins in New Orleans. After Mardi Gras they visited friends in Charleston, and when they returned to Toronto, Bill affected southern ways for a time. He appeared to admire a particular kind of southern gentleman who might in fact have never existed except in people's imaginations. This person was a stern and honorable man in a white linen suit. After overseeing his plantation with a firm but kind hand, he rocked on his veranda in the twilight and sipped bourbon and branch water. It was not surprising that *Gone with the Wind* was Bill Langford's favorite film.

And so, on returning from these winter sojourns, he was apt to greet Farris by standing over him and saying, "Now, Charlie, you sit right over there, you hear. I'm gonna make us a couple of fine big drinks and we're gonna sit out here by ourselves away from the womenfolk. Where the dickens have you been, boy? Have you been gallivanting around the country again writing those baseball stories?"

It was a harmless affectation, and, standing on the veranda on this late-fall day, Farris considered his debt of gratitude to Bill Langford and was glad finally that he had come. As he pressed the doorbell, he could see figures standing in the living room behind the curtains. When Pat opened the door, Farris was startled. She looked amazingly different, transformed by a new hairstyle. Her thick, dark helmet of hair had been severely cut and curled. She looked ten years younger.

"Hello, Charlie." He stepped inside and she took his hand. "I'm glad you came. I wasn't sure you would."

Not certain that he believed her, he said, "I'm glad I came, too."

This new look of hers was striking, and he must have stared at her, for she smiled and shyly touched her hair. "A little different, isn't it? I wanted a change. A new image."

In the old days she would have asked him if he liked it. He did, very much. But then why should she ask him now? She wasn't trying to make him like anything, and the realization nettled him. Pat took his coat and then, still holding his hand, led him toward the others. As they entered the room, he saw Neville watching them and Farris glared at the young man. Embarrassed, Neville turned away to talk to Mrs. Langford.

Farris surveyed the large room. Here the remnants of the family were assembled. Neville had now sat down next to Mrs. Langford and was trying to make conversation, though Farris doubted whether the old woman knew who he was or what he was talking about. Bill and Teddy and Sylvia stood talking to

Bunny Buckley, whose long, silvery hair flowed over his neck. Bill Langford broke away and came over to welcome Farris. He looked mildly bewildered in his large, baggy suit. "Charlie, I'm glad you could make it. How are you getting on?"

"I'm all right, Bill."

Warily Pat cocked an eye at the two of them while Bill gripped Farris's elbow. "How about a drink, Charlie? The others are having Bloody Marys. Or sherry." He looked at Pat. "Personally I don't care for Bloody Marys. The acid in the tomato juice gives me heartburn. It's not good on an empty stomach. How about joining me for a small whiskey, Charlie?"

"That's fine, Bill. Anything at all."

Pat looked skeptical. "Is that wise, Dad? You haven't had anything to eat today. Talk about acid on an empty stomach! What about whiskey?"

But Bill only patted her arm. "Now don't start fretting, Patty. You're just like your mother. I don't see Charlie every day." He hurried off to the dining room sideboard for the whiskey. Pat picked up her glass and, with her arms folded across her chest, she frowned at Farris as though she were regarding some mysterious stranger. "Dad always did like you, didn't he, Charlie? Even from the very first. The funny thing is I could never figure out why."

Farris looked her evenly in the eyes. "Thanks, Pat. You were always the flattering type."

She smiled a little. "No, wait, I didn't mean to insult you. It's just that you must admit most men don't like you. There's something about you that turns most men off. You seem to stand back and sneer."

"Guilty," he said.

"And you hate the hearty beer-commercial types, yet you've spent most of your life interviewing jocks. It's weird."

"Yes, it is," agreed Farris, "though you should never dismiss the ironic in life."

"Well, I think it's so strange that Dad . . . you know he's a club type. A backslapper. I mean, it's so strange that he should take to you. You two seem so different. Maybe that's it. But he talks about you all the time. Frankly, it's very annoying when Peter's around. Dad can be very insensitive. But I just don't understand this thing between you two."

"Maybe I listen to him," said Farris, watching her as she looked across the room at Neville. It annoyed him. She talked about her father's insensitivity, but she had a good measure of it, too. Pat suddenly turned back to him. "What? I'm sorry."

"Nobody ever listened to your father in this house." It was amazing how quickly they could anger one another, and now she looked offended and said quickly, "That's a crock of shit, Charlie, and you know it. You've never seen my father when he didn't have a drink in his hand. He can be a difficult man. When I was a kid I thought he was a tyrant. He's had his moments in this house, believe you me."

"So he's had his moments. I still like your old man. I always have."

"I wish you wouldn't call him that," she said stiffly.

"What?"

"My old man. It sounds . . . trashy."

Teddy looked over at them and lifted his glass in mock helplessness. He stood between Sylvia and Buckley and he looked bored and uncomfortable. His wife was an ex-Catholic and was forever struggling with her Anglicanism. Thus around Buckley she liked to discuss theology. In Farris's view, Buckley would have preferred to talk about football; he and Bill Langford had played college ball together and Buckley was a fan who sometimes drove to Orchard Park on Sunday afternoons to watch the Bills, returning in time for seven o'clock evensong.

Bill returned with two large whiskeys and Pat squeezed both their arms. "You two be careful now. I'm going over to speak to Grandmother."

Farris watched her join Neville and the old woman. And then, as so often happened in the past, an uneasy silence fell between Farris and his father-in-law. They needed whiskey to prime their companionship, and so they worked on their drinks. Bill did not look at all well; his face was mottled and his breathing seemed labored.

"What do you think of that whiskey, Charlie?" he asked. "Isn't that something? Pure malt. I bought a case last summer just before they hiked the price. It's a terrible price now." He looked at his glass with a gloomy eye. "I've got a case of the goddamn stuff and now I'm not supposed to drink it." He drained his glass in anger.

Teddy joined them. "I'm going to get another drink before we eat, Dad. Hello, Charlie."

"Well, hurry up, Teddy," said his father, who now appeared balky and bad-humored. "I think Miriam's about ready for us." But Farris was suddenly anxious. It was all wrong to be here, and he felt he should put down his glass and flee. All this seemed superfluous and wasteful. He was no longer a part of any of this. And suppose at this moment those people at the farm were deciding to get out and perhaps go to Florida or Mexico. Immediately he asked his father-in-law for another whiskey. To his surprise, Bill was mildly reluctant. "All right, but don't bring your glass to the table, Charlie. Pat hates that. She's just like her mother. Listen, why don't you go over and talk to Bunny? That man has been a fantastic help to

us this week." He left abruptly with Farris's glass. In
her pale-blue smock, Miriam was already putting
food on the table. Steam rose from plates and the air
was scented with the smell of coffee. Sylvia beckoned
to him and Farris went over to her and Buckley, who
stood by the fireplace. Buckley pressed Farris's hand.
"My dear Charles, how are you?"

"Managing, thanks." In all these years he had never known how to address John Buckley. "Father"
seemed too formal, yet the family name, Bunny, had
always struck Farris as preposterous. As usual, Sylvia
kissed his cheek, and continued to talk about the
Mass while Farris waited for his whiskey. Sylvia,
good-natured and guileless, prattled on about
changes in the liturgy. Her little daughters were now
watching TV cartoons in Bill's den and Farris
guessed that keeping the children out of sight was a
planned move. Nobody had yet mentioned the tragedy, but a sense of its awfulness pervaded the house
and colored everything. The writer watched a log
perish in the flames and reflected that tragedy im-
posed a new calendar on the lives of those afflicted.
From now on everything would be dated before or
after Jonathan's death. Their days would now be
drawn and measured from the events of last Saturday. As he looked around the room, Farris thought
of the contrast between this world and Donald
Stewart's. By now that pitiful young man would be
starting again in some seedy room in the Broughton
and Pendrell area of Vancouver. And what of the
murderers? What of the persons, wherever they were,
who had brought this family together to mourn? How
were they passing this first Saturday after the crime?
Were they remorseful? Frightened? Sick at heart?
Surely they could derive no feeling of triumph from
killing a child! Farris thought he could understand a

certain kind of criminal mentality taking pride in robbing a bank and escaping. But Jonathan's murder was such an iniquitous act. By any standard in any society it was monstrous.

He had closed his eyes against the firelight, which seemed to hold him in a hypnotic daze. He felt himself sweating again, and then perhaps he swayed a little, for Bunny Buckley was gripping his arm. "Did you say monsters, Charles?" Farris opened his eyes, and saw the priest's large, florid face and the richly flowing hair. "Are you all right, Charles?" asked Buckley.

"Fine thanks, yes."

Sylvia was looking at him in alarm, and it came to Farris that they probably thought he was drunk. "I'll be all right," he said. "A little dizzy there. The heat."

"I see," said the priest, smiling at him. Smug bastard, thought Farris as Bill came by with the whiskey. The maid was now whispering to Pat, who nodded and then helped old Mrs. Langford to her feet.

"Miriam says breakfast is ready, everybody. Let's eat while the food is hot."

Farris downed his whiskey in one swallow and watched Bunny Buckley's pitying glance. Farris grinned hideously at him, and the priest paled at the malice in the writer's face.

At the long table he sat at one end with Bill at the other. It was just like the old days. On either side of him were old Mrs. Langford and Teddy. Bunny Buckley said grace, and then the food was passed around. Conversation turned on the dark, scowling Miriam, who had gone to the kitchen. "I don't know how I'd get along without that girl," said Bill. "She bullies me all the time, but I couldn't do without her. Will you look at those eggs?"

"I wish I could get my eggs to look like that," said Sylvia to no one in particular.

Chewing his food, Teddy said, "I wish you could too."

There was a stack of toast, unbuttered, English-style, and platters of sausages and bacon with Mexican tomatoes. In the middle of the table was an immense bowl of scrambled eggs, and a large salver of home-fried potatoes. Beside Farris, Lavinia Langford heaped food on her plate lkke a greedy child. She seemed still to have a prodigious appetite. Farris watched the old woman as she worked at her task; the large, heavily veined hands looked like talons as they clutched the knife and fork. At one time she had been a great beauty, a writer of romantic fictions, and a sportswoman. It was said that in her fifties she played an exhibition match against the famous Babe Didrikson and lost by only a few strokes. Now she was a mere old ruin who might well see a hundred. As if reading his thoughts, the old woman looked up and peered at Farris. He could have been a stranger she was trying to place. "I'm ravenous, aren't you?" she said and returned to her food.

"How are you feeling, Grandma Langford?" asked Farris. She stared up at him again, cocking her head to one side like an old turkey hen. Her yellowing eyes glittered. "Why, this is Charles, Patricia's husband." She reached over and felt his arms. How these Langfords loved to lay hands upon you! thought Farris. "How are you, young man?"

"I'm fine, thank you, Grandma."

She wiped her lips with an enormous napkin and addressed Bill at the other end of the table. "Willy! You never told me that Patricia's Charles was taking breakfast with us."

Bill sipped his coffee. "He always comes to our

breakfasts, Mother. You know that."

"Do I indeed? Well, you might have told me." She turned again to Farris and patted his arm. "Well, it's very nice to see you again, Charles."

Farris looked down the table toward Pat, who was not eating. Her hands were in her lap and her face looked cold and stony. Beside her Neville picked at his food while Bunny Buckley asked him questions about educational television. Sylvia wanted to know about the Cayman Islands, but nobody seemed interested in telling her. Clearly the meal was not going well. A palpable tension hung in the air like a bad smell and everyone seemed afraid that he would say the wrong thing first. Farris felt himself hot under the arms as he suffered another attack of anxiety. He was sure his face was flushed and shining. Teddy asked him something about the hockey season, and Farris heard himself saying that he didn't follow sports closely anymore; in fact, sports bored him. Teddy looked baffled and embarrassed while Farris stared down at his plate of food and felt mildly nauseated. It passed through his mind that, sitting here at this table, he could be having some kind of nervous collapse, an old-fashioned breakdown. It also occurred to him, however, that he might still be drunk. Perhaps last night's alcohol had not yet burned through his bloodstream. And then Mrs. Langford asked suddenly, "And where are the children?"

Sylvia looked nervously at Pat and said, "They're watching television, Grandma." And then, as though summoned, the two little girls appeared in the dining room, standing by their mother's chair in dark-blue dresses and long white stockings. Their little buckled patent-leather shoes gleamed. But their faces were dark with anger and they glared at each other. One of them said, "Mother, Tracy won't let me watch 'Cartoon Playhouse.' She wants to watch some stupid program on figure skating."

Half-turning in his chair, Teddy said irritably, "Syl . . . will you get the kids out of here, please?"

"And where's the little boy?" asked Mrs. Langford. "Is he watching television too?"

"Yes, he is, Grandma," said Sylvia, getting up now to escort the children from the room. She looked around the table. "I'm sorry."

"I'm still hungry, Mother," said one of the little girls.

"Well that's all right," said Sylvia softly, "I'll bring you in some toast and jam."

"Oh, for crying out loud," said Teddy, looking at the ceiling. Although he sniffed a little coke and hobnobbed with gangsters, Teddy was still apt to use such expressions.

"Good heavens," said Lavinia Langford, "watching television while we're eating breakfast. I think that's disgraceful." She returned busily to her food. A terrible silence had fallen over the table, and the clatter of knives and forks against plates seemed embarrassingly loud. Then Pat suddenly arose and placed her balled-up napkin on the plate beside her. "Excuse me."

Half-rising in his chair, Neville said, "Darling?"

"No," she said fiercely and hurried from the room. Teddy watched her go and then put down his fork and knife and leaned forward on his elbows. He said to Farris, "Haven't they found out anything yet, Charlie? What the hell! Excuse me, Father, but what are they doing anyway? They've had a week."

"I don't know any more about it than you do, Ted," lied Farris. He could feel the sweat running down his spine. Neville spoke evenly as he smoothed out some wrinkles in the tablecloth with his butter knife. "The police told us that they have two hundred men working on this twenty-four hours a day."

Sylvia returned and sat down. "Thank God it's off the front page at last."

"I want to speak to that," said Bill. "This has been absolutely the worst thing that has ever happened to our family. But you've all been tremendous. . . ."

Farris watched the old lady next to him. Caught up in her appetite, she was oblivious to those around her.

"Well, let's just hope," continued Bill and stopped. He seemed to be groping for words. "Let's just hope that when they solve this thing, we can still maintain our dignity as a family."

"Amen," said Bunny Buckley.

"Well, I know how you feel about dignity, Dad," said Teddy. "And I agree with you about that, but I'm telling everyone right here and now that when they catch this guy, I intend to go to the trial. I don't care if it lasts six months and my business goes to pot, I'm still going to that trial. And I want a front seat, too, and I'm going to spend all my time just sitting there and staring at the bastard who did this. I want him to feel my eyes on him." He looked around, but no one spoke. "Of course, we know what will happen, don't we? Some damn psychiatrist will get up and testify that this . . . this creature is a victim of terrible circumstances, and he couldn't help what he was doing, blah blah blah. . . And then they'll give him a few years in some funny farm and he'll be out on the street ready to do it again."

"Well, maybe he *is* sick," said Sylvia. "I mean . . . anyone who would do such a terrible thing would have to be sick—"

"Sick my foot," cried Teddy. "It's people like you who make me sick talking that way."

"And what would you like to do, Ted?" asked Sylvia dryly. "Bring back public hanging? Chop off heads in Nathan Phillips Square?"

"Well, maybe I just would . . . in cases like this. . . ." Teddy floundered and looked around at the averted faces, aware now of how ridiculous he sounded. Bunny Buckley looked down at his plate.

"Please, Ted," said his father, "I think we've heard enough of that. This is a family meal and it's no place for quarrels."

Pat returned, her face scrubbed. With her curly cropped hair, she looked as solemn and undefiled as a convent girl. "Dad's right," she said, sitting down. "Let's at least try to be civil to one another."

Farris noted how she carried with her that same magisterial authority her mother had once brought to these occasions. He watched her as she reached for Neville's hand. Father Buckley returned to grilling Neville about educational TV and Mrs. Langford turned to Farris. "And do you watch much television, young man?" She seemed to have forgotten again who he was.

"Now and then, Grandma."

She nodded. "I watch that 'Sixty Minutes' program, but most television is rubbish, don't you think?"

"Yes, I do," said Farris. Miriam was now bending forward to collect the plates, her smooth brown face creased in a permanent frown. "Excuse me, ma'am," she said.

"Thank you," said the old lady, sitting back with her hands in her lap, childishly proud of her dinner plate, which had been polished with a piece of bread. Her oversized cup of hot water had been drained. Miriam removed the plates and Farris watched her sharp, angry profile at the sideboard. He would have enjoyed a cigarette, though one never smoked at this table. It used always to be one of the agonies of eating here. While Pat's mother presided over details of some family business, Farris and Pat had held hands under the table. Mrs. Langford would go on about some English cousin, who would be visiting Canada for the summer, and how everyone must do his best to make him welcome. And all this time Pat would be tickling Farris's palm like a lustful young high school girl. Later they held hands on the veranda and smoked Chesterfields smuggled across the border at Buffalo.

Now Teddy sat brooding beside him, and Sylvia, who could never get used to Miriam, was collecting side plates and stacking them. The conversation drifted around Farris, and he felt a tremendous desire to be on his way. He knew now that he would never again sit among these people at this table. This part of his life was over, and the idea of the impermanence of all things filled him with a peculiar sense of regret. A faintly pleasant sadness settled over him. Once he looked down the table directly at Pat, but she was listening to Neville and nodding in agreement. A moment later, Bunny Buckley announced that he had a three o'clock wedding and would have to be on his way. As if by signal everyone rose.

Farris and Teddy helped to settle Lavinia Langford on the sofa in the sitting room. She complained of the heat from the fireplace but would not consent to being moved away. As they left her, she abruptly released a high, squeaky fart. After hugging her father, Pat came into the sitting room looking somewhat distanced. Farris suspected it was the chemicals doing their job. Peter Neville stood beside her, and they both looked youthful and handsome. "Well, we're leaving now, Charlie. We have a million things to do before tomorrow." And was this it, then, he wondered. Now that Jonathan was gone, there was really no reason for them ever to have contact with one another again. To Farris it seemed brutally final. Pat leaned forward and brushed his cheek with her lips. "Good luck, Charlie."

Neville stuck out his hand and Farris shook it. Then they turned and were saying good-bye to Pat's grandmother, while Teddy came over to Farris. "Charlie? You take care of yourself, all right?"

"Yes, I'll do that, Ted."

"We'll have lunch together one of these days. When all this is over."

"Yes. Fine."

"I'll give you a call."

Teddy shook his hand and Sylvia put her slender arms around his neck. He felt her hard little breasts against his shirtfront. "I hope things work out for you, Charlie."

"Take care, Sylvia."

She made a sardonic face. "Oh, hell, our marriage has had it, Charlie. But I don't give a shit anymore." She looked around, but except for Farris no one was listening to her. "I'm sick of Teddy and I'm sick of the rest of them. I'm taking the kids and going back to Calgary one of these days. Be good to yourself, Charlie."

In the long dark hallway there was a brief commotion as the little girls pressed eagerly toward the door. Soon the front entrance was crowded and everyone was saying good-bye. In his topcoat Farris again shook hands with Teddy and the priest, but Bill Langford held his arm. "Just stay one minute, Charlie."

From the open door, Farris inhaled the pleasantly rank smell of damp leaves and cold ground. He stood next to Bill by the doorway and watched the others drive away. From behind car windows, arms were raised in farewell.

When everyone was out of sight, Bill closed the door and stared hard at Farris. "You look like hell, Charlie. Do you know that? I watched you in the dining room, and you hardly touched your food. When was the last time you sat down to a solid meal, anyway? From what I can see, about all you're doing these days is boozing. Now, a little booze is okay, especially during such a godawful time as this, but it can get to you." Bill's breath smelled bitter. "Do you know what, Charlie? I think you should go away and start over somewhere. That's what I'd do if I was your age. I'd get the hell away from here, because no matter how you cut it . . ." He lowered his head and shook it from side to side. His voice trembled. "We can't bring him back, can we?" From the kitchen came the sound of dishes being scraped and stacked. Reggae music drifted faintly from a radio.

"No, we can't bring him back, Bill," said Farris.

Wiping at his eyes, Bill walked to a small table and picked up a silver tray covered with cards and letters. He held it forth like an offering. "You should see some of these, Charlie. Many from people I haven't heard from or seen in years. People can really be very nice. . ."

"It's time I was going, Bill. Thanks for inviting me."

"Oh, sure. I was glad you could make it. I must have put you in an awkward spot here." He sighed. "Do you need any money or anything, Charlie? If you're short I could let you have a few hundred. I've got it right here in the house."

"No thanks, Bill."

From the sitting room old Mrs. Langford cried,

"Willy! Where are you now? Where has everyone gone?"

Bill looked down at the tray of cards. "I'm coming, Mother," he called angrily. Farris opened the door and stepped out onto the veranda. Down the street, two boys about Jonathan's age were throwing a football back and forth, their voices lifting and falling through the raw air. Farris shook Bill's hand. "You should lie down and have a rest, Bill. You look tired."

The older man nodded. "I am tired, Charlie. That's the truth."

"Good-bye, Bill," said Farris as he started down the steps. He was nearly to the sidewalk when Bill called after him, "You'll be all right, Charlie. Come and visit sometime. I'll hold you to that, now."

Without looking back, Farris waved and walked on toward his car, passing the big houses and the leafless trees and the boys at their game.

PART THREE

CHAPTER ONE

Before he left the city, Farris had the VW's oil checked and the gas tank filled. In a shopping plaza near the freeway he bought cigarettes and potato chips and a six-pack of beer. Two hours later he was a hundred miles east of Toronto and had thrown the last of the beer bottles out the window as he left the freeway and drove north on a narrow two-lane highway. In the failing gray light the countryside looked exhausted and desolate to Farris, who, though born in a small town, was a city man at heart. Yet inside the little car he felt self-contained and secure. The beer and potato chips had tasted good, and the warm, smoky air reminded him of car rides twenty years before when he had covered hockey games for a small-town newspaper and afterward had driven home along deserted highways like this. Also he was elated by the nature of this journey, and in spite of the beer felt light and quick, queerly at ease with himself and the world. If Donald Stewart had suckered him for a plane ticket to Vancouver and a thousand dollars, so be it. If, however, he was telling the truth and Farris would soon see his son's murderers, then so be that, too. And what then? Truthfully, he had given little thought to that. At the moment it seemed to him more a matter of intense curiosity. He was anxious to know what kind of a man would murder a child and cause so much grief.

He remembered feeling the same abiding curiosity a few years ago when he found himself in Niagara Falls, New York. He knew his first wife had remarried and was now living there, so he looked up her name in the phone book. And without so much as a telephone call, he went to see her. Darlene lived on a little street of frame bungalows. Nearby there were factories and the neighborhood had an unpleasantly sweet chemical smell to it. Farris hadn't seen his first wife in years, yet at one time she had been the most important person in his life. All through high school they had been inseparable. But when nineteen-year-old Farris told his mother that he was going to marry Darlene Haines, the woman sank to her knees and begged him not to get mixed up with such a family of heathens. Denied her blessing and hot-faced with embarrassment, Farris had slammed the door and broken a pane of glass on his way out of the house. At the wedding he was alone, except for the Haines family and their friends. Nearly everyone got drunk, and late in the evening Darlene's young brother, Billy, threatened to knock out Farris's teeth if Darlene was ever mistreated. There was a drunken reconciliation, and the couple drove away, headed for a hotel in Toronto. But neither of them could wait, so they stayed instead at a motel a few miles from town. And there, after years of frustrated constraint, scarcely believing that they were at last alone and naked together, they explored each other like children.

Working for the town weekly, Farris covered ball games and attended father-and-son banquets. In the evenings he read Thomas Hardy's novels to Darlene, extravagantly pleased when she appeared to enjoy a particular passage. But in fact, a month after their wedding he knew sorrowfully that she was only indulging him by listening; she really preferred Harlequin romances and *Photoplay* magazine. Sometimes when he arrived home in the late afternoon, she would be sitting in the darkened apartment above the furniture store watching game shows or old Westerns on their tiny black-and-white TV. When he took a better job in a nearby town, she came along. But her heart was not in the move, and, growing homesick, she eventually returned to live with her family. Mercifully their brief marriage had produced no children. So, curious to know what had become of his pretty, long-legged high school sweetheart, Farris had gone to the odorous little street and knocked on her front door. He recognized her at once when she stood behind the screen wearing jeans and a loose plaid shirt. Fleshier, and with her brown hair now Afroed, she was still a tremendously good-looking woman. She stood holding a hand against her eyes to shield them from the sun. Was he a salesman? And then she noticed him. "Why, Charlie! Why, for God sakes! What are you doing here?" Darlene had laughed uncomfortably, pressing splayed fingers against her chest. "Well, look at me! Why didn't you phone first?" She wasn't pleased by this surprise visit.

In the living room a little fair-haired boy in diapers sat cross-legged in front of a huge color TV console. And in a corner near a potted fern a beautiful blond girl-child, perhaps five years old, sucked her thumb and stared fiercely at Farris. All the time he was there she never uttered a word, nor would she venture forth despite her mother's entreaties. After a few minutes the little boy grew boisterous and from time to time interrupted his mother while she reminisced about old times. Never scolding, Darlene talked around the child as he leaned across her knees and over her shoulder. There was no beer in the house, so she mixed rum and Cokes and talked about the fates of old high school friends Farris could no longer remember. As she summoned forth obscure names from their past, he tried to fit them into his memory. But it was a hopeless task, and he felt vaguely ashamed for having so thoroughly discarded his youth. Darlene, however, still kept in touch with old girl friends, and as she talked Farris stared hard at this middle-aged stranger he had once loved. She was now married to a fireman, a Vietnam veteran she met on a trip to Disneyland. She showed Farris a picture of him on vacation somewhere. The man looked beefy and tough in his open-neck short-sleeve shirt and checkered slacks. Darlene said she enjoyed living in the States. Things were cheaper, but there were too many coloreds and that took some getting used to, though she had nothing against them personally. When Farris rose to leave, his fantastic and greedy curiosity finally satisfied, Darlene pressed him to stay for dinner, though he knew she didn't mean it. They were both relieved when he was on his way. It was odd to be thinking of Darlene Haines as he approached the outskirts of Poulton. But then maybe not so odd, since small towns like Poulton have a way of reviving memories for middle-aged Canadians like Farris who grew up in them.

It was now nearly four o'clock and on this overcast afternoon darkness was probably less than an hour away. Donald Stewart had said the farm was about five miles north of the town, so Farris guessed he would reach it in fifteen minutes or so. There would be time to have a look before dark. Poulton looked much the same as dozens of other small Ontario towns, with the highway bisecting it and becoming the main street. Before reaching downtown, however, the highway passed a cemetery and, farther along, a few gas stations and fast-food restaurants. On the left was a new subdivision. In the older part of town there were large brick and white frame houses set back on spacious lawns. On corners squatted the homely red brick United and Presbyterian churches. The main street was three blocks long, with its rows of stores and its town hall and Carnegie Library. Overhead Christmas lights had been strung across the street and Christmas music came from a loud-speaker over a furniture store selling radios and stereos. The town was busy with shopping families, and Farris had trouble finding a parking space on the main street. But after a few minutes he parked on a side street near the liquor store. There he bought three bottles of scotch and returned to the car.

Excited now and apprehensive, he had to stop on the outskirts of town to take a long piss, his water steaming into the dead weeds by the roadside. A passing car filled with young people honked approval. Inside the VW again, Farris opened one of the bottles and drank some whiskey. It made his eyes water and for a moment he coughed violently, but the liquor steadied his nerves as he put the car in gear. A mile or so beyond town he passed a small, clean-looking motel tucked in behind some pine trees. It looked like a good place to take a girl and a bottle of whiskey, and he wished now that he had phoned Madeline Greene to apologize for whatever it was he had said to her last night.

The highway continued north for another few miles and then ended abruptly at a huge flashing stop sign. Here was Highway 7, the province-wide road linking Sarnia in the west with Ottawa in the east. Following Donald Stewart's instructions, Farris turned left. The surrounding land looked too poor to cultivate; it was mostly brushland and fir trees, though here and there he saw a farm at the end of a long empty lane, the barn lights already burning as the farmer got on with his evening chores. And then, with mounting anxiousness, Farris saw the small township sign for the Ninth Line. He slowed and turned right onto a gravel road badly pitted by autumn rains. Narrow and winding, the road descended into several small valleys, always rising to crest yet another hill. And on top of one such hill, Farris's heart contracted as he faced suddenly a mud-spattered pickup truck hogging the road at fifty miles an hour. He caught only a glimpse of the driver, an open-mouthed farm boy with his girl friend squeezed next to him, as they hurtled past with only inches to spare. A shower of stones was flung against the Volkswagen as a shaken and cursing Farris slowed to a crawl. Then, at the bottom of a long hill, he saw a road to the left and here again he turned. So far it was just as Stewart had described. On both sides of the road was bush and, if the boy was to be believed, this opened onto cleared fields and a farm a few hundred yards along. Farris drove now at a moderate speed; he did not want to attract attention by driving too slowly, though he guessed any strange car would be noticed on a country road.

The farm was there all right, an unpainted wooden house at the end of a long lane. A black high-wheeled truck was parked near an outbuilding. As he passed the place, Farris saw the word *Hanlon* on the mailbox, though the name had been almost erased by the weather. Farther along he stopped on the shoulder of the road and took another drink. Now that he was here, he had to do something. He lit a cigarette and decided that the best course was simply to drive into the farm and see for himself. He could recognize them if they were there. And if they weren't and this was a hoax, then at least he'd be done with it, and he could go back to that motel and get drunk. He would drive into the farm and ask for directions; he could say he had lost his way and wanted to get back on the highway. They wouldn't know him from Adam. After another drink, he turned the car around and started back toward the farm. The windshield was now slowly beading with rain and Farris again felt foolish. Here he was on a godforsaken backwoods road playing detective. He had always hated melodrama, yet now he sensed that he was a part of one. He touched his hot face with a shaking hand.

The lane was almost a narrow path overgrown with high gray weeds that brushed the sides of the car. Clearly this was no working farm, and as he drew nearer, Farris saw further evidence of ruin and abandonment. Still visible was the stone foundation of a barn that had probably burned long ago. An old wooden implement shed stood apart from the house, down a sloping lawn. The house itself looked derelict, though a single light shone through a downstairs window. To Farris it looked like the kind of place dissatisfied city dwellers might retreat to on a weekend. Or a place where bikers cooked up speed and banged their girl friends silly. And then ahead of him, near the corner of the house, a Doberman suddenly ran out of the bad light and lunged at the end of a chain, its hoarse bark carrying across the fields. Farris tightened his grip on the wheel and thanked God he was inside the car. Stewart hadn't mentioned any dog, let alone a fucking Doberman. The animal appeared crazed at the sight of the Volkswagen and, rearing up on its hind legs, nearly strangled itself against the taut chain. Its fearful racket followed Farris as he drove alongside the black and silver Chevy Cheyenne. He noted the license number as he backed up and wheeled around to face the dog, who advanced to within five feet of the car. Farris could see now that the dog's chain allowed him to patrol the area near the entrance to the house.

A tall, thin man had come out the side door and now stood on the sagging veranda by an old sofa. Farris shakily lit a fresh cigarette off an old one and watched the man approach the car through the drizzle. Farris guessed he was about thirty. With his long, bony face, and in jeans and boots and leather vest, he could easily have passed for some small-time country singer. His blond hair was pulled back in a ponytail. In fact, Snapshot looked exactly as Stewart had described him and Farris felt choked with excitement. The Doberman leaped wildly toward the man, who cuffed it across the snout with an open hand. He then leaned over and, grabbing the dog's collar, unfastened the yard chain. Holding the dog on a two-foot leash, he walked toward the Volkswagen. Farris willed himself to be calm and rolled the window down.

"Excuse me, but I'm turned around," he said. He wondered if his voice sounded right. "I'm trying to get back on Number 7." The Doberman strained at the leash, and at the sound of Farris's voice began again to bark. "You shut up now," said the man, knocking his fist gently against the dog's head. He looked blankly at Farris and then pointed toward the road. He sounded friendly enough. "That way you come from. That's the way back to the highway." Farris had an ear for voices, but he couldn't place this one. It sounded like a mildly affected drawl. Like a man imitating an Oklahoma cowboy.

"You mean I go back the way I came from?" asked Farris. He tried to sound bewildered.

"That's right, man." Snapshot had now lifted his face to the dark gray sky and closed his eyes as though the rain offered refreshment. Then, like a man clearing his head, he opened his eyes again and looked at Farris. "Where are you coming from, anyways?"

Farris glanced up at the pale heavy face above him. "Well, I've been out all afternoon looking at places. Thinking I might buy something around here. For the summer, I mean. I've been all back through these parts, and to tell you the truth, I'm really confused." The man again pointed down the lane. Beside him the dog now sat still as a statue with its ears cocked.

"Well, look, man, it's simple. You just go back down that road. What happened is you must have turned right instead of going straight when you come down the hill. What you got to do now is go out our lane here and turn right. Then go to that stop sign and turn right again. That's the Ninth Line, and that takes you right out to Number 7. You made a turn on the Ninth Line when you should have kept going straight."

"Yes," said Farris. "I got confused. I should have kept going straight on that hill, right?"

"That's exactly right." Farris couldn't be sure, but the man appeared to be slightly drunk or drugged. He smiled down at Farris. "I'm sorry about the dog. He's not used to strangers."

"That's all right," said Farris. He put the car in gear. "Thanks for your help."

Snapshot stepped back and waved. "That's all right, man. No problem."

Farris moved slowly down the laneway while the

man led the dog toward the house. Behind the curtains on the kitchen window, figures moved, and Farris was almost certain he saw two faces peering out at the car. One of them wore glasses and looked like Marty Poole.

On the road again, Farris was afraid for his heart. He was shaking so with excitement that he feared a coronary. The bastards were at the farm all right. That wretched young man had spoken the truth, and, holding up the whiskey bottle, Farris drank a long toast to Donald Stewart. On the right-hand side of the road he noticed a small clearing in the bush. It looked like an old trail, probably now used only by lovers or hunters. Farris stopped the car. He needed time to think. He could reach that motel in fifteen minutes and phone Grahame. The detective would think he was crazy or drunk, but by now Grahame would follow any lead. He would get in touch with the local cops, and within the hour the provincial police would be at the farm. Yet Farris was reluctant to leave his quarry now that he had tracked them down. What if they were now preparing to leave? But then he had the truck's license number, didn't he?

Confused and strangely depressed, he backed the VW onto the old road and stopped thirty feet into the bush. When he turned off the ignition, he heard only the cooling tappets ticking away and then the fall of freezing rain around him. Rolling down the window, he listened to the stuff hitting the dead leaves on the ground and pinging against the car. He rolled up the window and took another drink, reflecting that he had drunk whiskey in strange places, but never in the middle of an Ontario bush in freezing rain. As he looked up through the trees, he saw the last of the day's light expire, and felt the darkness close around him. From time to time he turned on the motor to keep warm. Once he heard a car traveling fast along the township road, and he strained to hear the sound as it faded and then vanished beyond another hill. Cautioning himself not to get drunk, he was nevertheless alarmed when he held the bottle against the windshield and saw how little was left. And then within him arose bitter suspicions about his ability ever to get anything right. In a crucial situation you could always count on Charlie Farris. To get drunk. He had tracked down these bastards and now he was sitting a few hundred yards away getting loaded. He had seen the face of the man who had raped and murdered his son. That heavy, pale, smart-ass face. He had even talked to him. And what was it he had said to Farris? *No problem, man.* Farris trembled with rage. The lying, murdering bastard. *No problem, man.* Stuffing the bottle into his topcoat, Farris opened the door and felt the shock of icy rain on his head.

CHAPTER TWO

He was indeed half-drunk, as he discovered when he stood pissing by the side of the car amid tin cans and rotting cardboard boxes. This primitive trail led only to some farmer's dump. The cold, soaking rain was dispiriting, but the air revived him and cleared his head. The trees were now slippery with ice and the Volkswagen was coated. Turning his collar up, Farris walked to the main road and made his way toward the farm. Near the laneway, he climbed a wire fence and dropped into a field. He had in mind to approach the farmhouse by this field, which ran parallel to the lane. Once Farris was beyond the house, he would turn right and come up behind the old implement shed. From there he could cross the farmyard and get a closer look. He was guessing and hoping that they would keep the Doberman indoors on such a dirty night. If they didn't he was in serious trouble, and as he walked through the field he looked around half-heartedly and in vain for some kind of weapon. He regretted, too, not having a hat. Already his hair was matted with ice and water ran down his neck and face. His feet were also cold in street shoes. Underfoot, the ground was greasy with rain, and once he fell as he descended a knoll. Old cow dung encrusted with ice broke under his shoes. Through the rain he could now see the kitchen light in the farmhouse, and nearer to him the dark shape of the implement shed. The freezing rain was soaking him through. He hadn't believed he could be this cold, and he realized that he must get out of this weather or he would perish. His teeth were now chattering and his hands felt numb.

At the back of the shed he almost impaled himself on the spikes of an old harrow half-buried in long grass and weeds. The metal was freezing to the touch. Holding on to the sides of the shed, Farris groped his way around to the front, where he found a sliding door rusted open. The entrance was little more than a foot wide, and he squeezed through, grateful at last to be out of the desolating rain. The musty building was filled with old lumber, and in one corner Farris discerned the outline of an ancient horse sleigh. After unbuttoning his coat, he warmed his hands in his armpits and then drank some whiskey. Through the open doorway he could see the truck and the house perhaps three hundred feet away. Now and then a figure passed by the kitchen window. Between the house and Farris was an outdoor toilet on the edge of what looked like a small orchard. Farris stood by the narrow opening, and then retreated within to smoke a cigarette, noting dismally that he had only one more left in the package.

Back at the doorway, he again surveyed the bleak scene. There was no sign of the Doberman, though Farris knew that he was still too far away for the animal to notice him. He decided that his next move must be to the outdoor toilet, and that would determine whether the beast was on patrol or not. Farris again squeezed through the doorway and, bending low, began a crablike run toward the outhouse. By now the grass was like a skating rink, and twice he lost his footing and fell to the freezing ground. Grunting with the effort, he finally reached the remnants of a vegetable garden and here, after stepping through rotted squash and tomatoes, he gained the outhouse. As he pressed himself against the rough wood, he heard only the dense sound of the rain and the limbs of apple trees nearby cracking under their burden of ice.

Inside the cold, stale little toilet he sat down and blew hard on his hands, flexing the stiffened fingers. In the darkness he could see a roll of toilet paper, and on the floor he touched newspapers and magazines and an old broken garden rake. Leaning forward, he set the door ajar a few inches and saw the veranda of the house perhaps a hundred and fifty feet away. With the toilet paper he dried off his face and wiped his hair. After two long drinks he lit his last cigarette, holding it cupped in his hands. Conscious of the absurdity of his situation, he leaned forward and watched the house, sipping whiskey from time to time and slowly smoking his cigarette. Once he hiccupped from cold and nervousness and the sound startled him. The heavy rain, now almost hail, drummed against the roof of the little building and the damp, cold air streamed through the doorway.

When he finished his cigarette, he struck a match and examined the pile of newspapers and magazines at his feet. The Toronto newspapers were several months old, and there were also faded copies of the *National Enquirer*. Underneath these he fished out a grimy magazine filled with pictures of nude boys. Lighting another match, he looked closely at the photographs of young men in lewd postures, some fingering immense erect penises and other submitting to fellatio and sodomy. Many of the pages were crusted together, and Farris suspected it was from dried semen. Someone had masturbated in front of these cheerless photographs. Dropping the magazine onto the pile, he again looked out at the house. He felt a sudden and extraordinary depletion of spirit. That his son had died in such corrupt circumstances and at the hands of such iniquitous persons was ruinously depressing. In the smelly, cold toilet the writer wept. A hysterical grief seemed to grip his heart and he covered his mouth to keep from crying out. The filthy murdering bastards. Sobbing, he covered his face in his hands, only to jerk upright as he heard a dog bark.

Yellow light now flooded across the lawn near the veranda, and Farris watched Snapshot release the Doberman. From the open kitchen door came country music. The big dog bounded forth, barking excitedly. But when it reached the icy grass, it lost its balance and skidded comically sideways. On the veranda Snapshot laughed and drank from a beer bottle. Clearly the Doberman did not like the weather and stood only a few feet from the house, barking and awaiting the call to return. After a while it trotted off and sniffed along the grass before lifting its leg by a bush. A heavyset figure in bib overalls and flat cap had joined Snapshot on the veranda, and they both watched the Doberman as it tried for purchase on the coated grass. The figure could have been a man, but Farris knew it was Mrs. Poole. She carried something in her arms, and when she knelt down, Farris saw that it was of all things a white poodle. The little animal yapped at the wet night, but would not venture beyond the veranda. Instead it squatted by the old sofa to make its water, and then Mrs. Poole picked it up again and carried it into the house. When Snapshot whistled for the Doberman, it came scrabbling across the lawn and onto the veranda. A moment later the light went out, and Farris took another swallow of whiskey. He was shivering badly with cold and fear. A long moment passed, and he watched the rain turn to wet, heavy snow. It fell thick and fast and Farris stood up. He would need some kind of weapon.

The veranda light had come on again and the screen door banged. Farris heard a youthful voice calling out something about the snow. Leaning forward, he saw Marty Poole standing on the veranda with his arms raised to the sky like a prophet.

"Hey, everybody. It's snowing out here. Everything looks really neat. Hey, Mom . . . Snapshot. You should see the snow."

The names had at least been uttered, and at his ignoble post Farris groaned with relief. Then another voice, severe and hectoring, carried across the farmyard. "Marty . . . you be careful out there. You'll catch your death of cold."

"I won't be long," cried the young man as he took a run and then a tremendous slide along the grass, falling finally in laughter.

"Hey, this is fun," he called as he got to his feet.

"You get the hell out of that snow, Marty, you hear me." She might have been talking to a child. The young man threw a snowball at the house. "I'll be back in a minute. I have to go to the john." And the woman's voice boomed forth again. "Well, get out of that snow for Christ sakes, you're not dressed for it."

Marty Poole was still sliding along as he made his way across the yard toward Farris. He was laughing and holding out his arms at his sides like a high-wire man. In the toilet Farris waited, appalled by the young man's laughter. In both fists he had doubled the ends of his belt, so that he now held a kind of garroting loop about two feet in length. As the young man drew near, Farris pressed back against the corner, reminding himself to watch his head as the door opened. When it did, Farris held the loop against his chest and waited for the door to close. Poole's back was to him, and Farris noted with pleasure that the young man was several inches shorter. When Farris slipped the belt around Poole's throat and pulled, he felt the young man buckle with surprising ease. His hands clawed at the leather. Of course, it would be a terrible surprise, an utter shock to both mind and body. What must be going through the young man's head as he was assaulted thus in a stinking shithouse in the middle of a snowstorm? Farris was surprised at his calm deliberations. He had never done anything remotely like this before, yet it seemed easy. Poole's arms flailed the air and then returned again to his collared throat. One leg shot up against the back wall and the little outhouse rocked ominously. Farris kicked him behind the knee, and Poole collapsed to the floor. After loosening the belt, Farris straddled the young man, leaning hard against his chest and gripping the collar of his Windbreaker. In the struggle Poole had lost his glasses and, looking up now aghast, saw only a figure in a light coat bearing down upon him. Astride the youth, Farris tightened his hold on the Windbreaker. He could just make out the face below him, round and fat and pale as a little moon. Beneath him he could feel the young man's thudding heartbeat. He whispered at the face, "You're Marty Poole, aren't you? Just move your fucking head yes or no." The boy frantically moved his head up and down.

"Your mother and Snapshot are inside the house.

Is there anyone else in there?" The head wagged from side to side. With his left hand Farris grasped Poole's hair, pulling it back against the pile of newspapers. "Now in a minute I'm going to take my hand off your throat, cocksucker. But only for a minute. If you scream, I'll fucking choke you to death right here. Do you understand?" Again there was the same furious nodding. Farris slowly eased his right hand from the boy's collar and Poole coughed. Farris looked down at him. "You and that bastard Snapshot raped and murdered Jonathan Farris, didn't you? Last Saturday night, just a week ago." Farris thought he could now see tears glistening in the boy's eyes. With his damaged windpipe, Poole's voice was a mere hoarse whisper. "Who are you?"

Farris slammed his forearm into the boy's throat. "Don't ask questions, you little fuck. You and Snapshot killed Jonathan Farris, didn't you?"

Marty Poole's face was wet with tears, and Farris leaned harder against him.

"Snapshot met him in the park last Saturday afternoon and then they went back to your old lady's house, didn't they? And you all decided to have a little party. Maybe give the kid a joint and then play around a little. Take few dirty pictures and then maybe have a little bum fuck. Right? Only things got out of hand and the boy wouldn't go along with it, would he? He got scared, but that didn't matter to you and Snapshot. You wanted your tail and you were going to get it whether the kid liked it or not. So you fucked him and killed him. Right?"

He relaxed the pressure against Poole's throat. "Am I right so far?" The boy's mouth opened and he whispered, "I'm sorry."

Farris grabbed the throat again and felt a rush of

blood to his own head. It was almost dizzying. "Sorry!" He was no longer whispering. "You fucking liar. You killed my son one week ago tonight and just a few minutes ago you were laughing and singing and fucking around in the snow. Don't give me that 'sorry' shit. While my son rots in the ground, you slide on the fucking ice and laugh. And you tell me you're fucking sorry."

Marty Poole gasped for air. "It was Snapshot," he whispered. "Snapshot did it."

"And you watched him, didn't you? You helped to hold him down. Donald Stewart told me everything, you bastard. And your old lady is in on it too, isn't she? She helped to get rid of the body, didn't she? She helped Snapshot wrap my son in a fucking garbage bag and then dumped him behind a factory like a pile of shit."

Something struck him on the side of the head, and for an instant Farris feared the loss of his left eye. It was filling with fluid, and when he put his hand to his head he felt the wetness and knew it was blood. There followed another blow against his forehead, and he dimly realized that Poole had worked his right arm free and was swinging the handle of the garden rake at him. Yet another blow struck Farris's cheekbone and the pain was terrible. He thought he must have blacked out for a second, for he found himself on his hands and knees holding on to one of Marty Poole's legs. Poole was now on his feet, trying to tug open the door. His bowels had loosened in fear and Farris could smell him. With his free leg the boy kicked at Farris and the writer lost his grip. As he reached out again, he felt a fingernail shred against the young man's jeans.

But Farris caught up with him a few yards from the

toilet and they fell together in the snow. Poole cried for his mother, but his voice was gone. He had risen to his hands and knees when Farris, remembering to close his eyes smashed the whiskey bottle against the boy's face. Bits of glass stung Farris's face and for a moment the smell of whiskey filled the air. When Farris opened his eyes, Marty Poole was lying in the snow. Farris bent over him and saw the shattered face leaking blood and heard the quick, shallow breathing. Crouched beside the dying boy, Farris felt only the snow soaking his head and the trembling in his arms.

At the farmhouse the veranda light illuminated the heavy, fast snowfall, and with his good eye Farris saw Mrs. Poole looking out at the night. She was calling for her son. "Marty!" The voice came through the falling snow. "What the hell are you doing out there? Get in here now." Farris knew she couldn't see them, yet he hunkered down into the snow like a fugitive. "Marty!" called his mother. "You answer me now, goddamn it." Then she returned to the house and Farris guessed she was getting a coat and boots. Beside him the boy shuddered and died. He waited for panic to seize him. He had just killed a man, and he knew that from this moment his own life would be forever changed. But except for a ringing in his ears, he felt calm enough. However, the woman would soon be coming and he knew he would have to move away from here.

He ran across the snowy farmyard toward the old shed, but Mrs. Poole saw him as she came down the veranda steps. She was wearing long rubber boots and pulling on a coat, and when she saw the running man she shouted after him, "Hey you! What are you doing out there?" Her voice was edged with fear, and again she called for her son. When Farris reached the shed, he heard her shouting, "Snapshot! There's somebody out here. Something's going on. Get the dog." Inside the shed Farris heard the Doberman, and the panic finally flooded through him. Crying now with fear, he leaned against the old sliding door, straining to close it. After a moment it did move slowly along its rusted track a few inches. But it refused to shut entirely and Farris turned from it and stared wildly into the damp darkness around him. He could hear Snapshot yelling, "What the fuck is going on?" And Mrs. Poole, now excited and frightened, shouted, "There's a man in the shed, I think. Where's Marty?"

In the shed Farris slowly made his way toward the old horse sleigh in the corner, his hands feeling the rough wood of the wall. Then one of his hands touched metal and something fell and clattered against the stone floor. He stooped to pick it up, and in his right fist hefted an old sickle that had been hanging on a nail. The Doberman's excited barking drew nearer, and then as Farris turned, he saw the dog's long head and shoulders plunging through the narrow opening. But it was a tight squeeze, and the baffled, madly barking dog wriggled to free itself. Bracing himself, Farris brought the sickle down hard across the dog's muzzle. As the sickle struck flesh and bone, the dog howled terribly and wriggled backwards. Again Farris brought down the sickle and the terrified animal, pulling free at last from the doorway, began a grotesque dance in the snow. Dropping to its stomach, the Doberman pawed at its torn face. Then it rolled over and got up to trot a few steps before falling. At the doorway of the shed Farris watched the animal describe a circle in the bloodied snow. And not twenty feet away, Snapshot watched too and then said, "Jesus Christ Almighty," and turned toward the house. Farris watched him run up the slope of the yard. He stumbled several times as he fled. Then Farris heard Mrs. Poole's screams.

CHAPTER THREE

The woman's screams unsettled him. This ancient sound of grief and suffering was utterly terrifying, and as Farris walked toward her, he was badly frightened. She was kneeling beside her son's body when she looked up and saw Farris standing by the corner of the toilet. He waited for her as she rose and ran toward him with arms outstretched and a great cry of rage in her throat. The sickle rested easily in his right hand and he thought of sidestepping her and striking a blow as she went past. But with only one good eye he misjudged her speed and was startled when she bolted into him. As he fell backwards his head struck the side of the outhouse and the sickle flew from his hand. Then he felt Mrs. Poole's fingers seeking purchase on his throat. Oddly enough she still wore the flat cap, but he saw only its outline as he struggled beneath her weight. With his right hand he punched her face again and again, and smelled blood and stale liquor. He had squeezed his legs tight against one of her hands, which grabbed for his genitals. Above him she cursed and sobbed and finally, to escape his fist, buried her face in his stomach. Farris partly rose and then screamed as the woman sank her teeth into his thigh. She was trying desperately to pry open his legs, but she stopped when he pinched her eye and felt it give way beneath his fingers. Moaning, she put her hands to her face, and Farris struggled to his feet. Across the yard he could just make out Snapshot running toward the truck.

On her feet again, Mrs. Poole prepared to attack, lowering her head like a beast. Farris snatched up the garden rake, which was lying near the toilet door. As she came toward him, he thrust the broken end through her neck, amazed at how easily it entered the flesh. The big woman staggered backwards and then fell absurdly to a sitting position in the snow. There she sat tugging at the rake handle in her throat while Farris, on hands and knees in the muddy snow, searched for his sickle. He heard the truck motor cough into life, and wished that he had remembered to flatten the tires. He cursed his stupidity.

When he found the sickle, he felt better, though the wound in his thigh throbbed and made walking painful. Mrs. Poole had now leaned forward and with her right hand was scratching the ground beside her convulsively, stirring the muddied snow. A great issue of blood poured from her mouth to darken the snow between her legs. On the veranda the poodle was yapping at Snapshot, who had driven the truck into a fence post near the house. He was standing by the truck, clawing at the iced windshield. But Farris guessed that by now the ice was at least a quarter of an inch thick, and even with a scraper, it would take twenty minutes to clear that glass. Perhaps his enemy thought so too, for he suddenly abandoned his task and ran for the house. The little dog barked frantically as the man ran past him. He would be terrified, thought Farris, and that was good. His mind would be totally foxed. There was a maniac loose in the barnyard.

Yet Farris doubted that he was crazy. In any case, he knew he would never plead madness in a courthouse, though Bill Langford would hire lawyers who would insist that this was the only thing to do. The father, maddened by grief, slays his son's killers. They would call on Toomey, who would diagnose a post-bereavement reactive state. Or whatever. In vain he would tell them that he had murdered these people without pity or remorse, and in the full knowledge that he was committing a grievous wrong in the eyes of the law. But they would regard that only as further evidence of his madness. For the next few years he would play softball and floor hockey with the other crazies up at Oak Ridges.

On the veranda it passed through his mind that Snapshot might have returned to the house for a weapon, perhaps a gun. It was conceivable that such people would have a gun on the premises. And then, incredibly enough, as he looked through the window he saw Snapshot holding a rifle. He was also swallowing some pills, holding his head back to get them down without water. The gun looked like a .22 groundhog rifle and Snapshot was having trouble loading it, as his shaking hands spilled shells onto the floor. Farris was enormously pleased that it wasn't a shotgun. A shotgun would have been difficult. For reasons best known to himself, or simply because of panic, the man had left the door unlocked, and when Farris walked into the kitchen, Snapshot looked up with wide eyes. On the radio some country singer was lamenting his lonely life in the city. "What the fuck do you want, man? You get away from here." Snapshot sounded horrified. The kitchen smelled of sour dishes and the dogs. Farris guessed that if he wasn't hit in the head or the heart, he could survive a bullet or two and reach the man, who was now waving the rifle and shouting in a high voice. "Listen, man, you come any closer now and I'll blow your fucking head off. I mean it, you crazy bastard. What the fuck do you want anyway?"

They circled an old wooden table with the tall, frightened man waving his rifle but retreating. Farris held his left arm in front of him and was grateful that Snapshot wouldn't shut up. He recalled once watching a cowardly man provoke a fight in a tavern and then back away like this, talking all the time. "I'm warning you, man. Just fuck off. Drop that goddamn thing or I'm going to shoot you. It's self-defense." Farris suspected the goof balls were doing their work and it would soon be too late. He heaved his weight against the table, pushing Snapshot back against an old yellowed refrigerator. Then, as he came around the table, he heard several clicks and a loud report. He smelled the burned gunpowder and opened his eyes to swing his weapon. The pain rang through his right arm as the sickle struck the refrigerator. Snapshot pressed the trigger again and again, but the rifle was either jammed or empty. Cursing, he wielded it now like a club. "I'm going to kill you, you bastard." He seemed suddenly enraged.

Farris guessed he'd been shot somewhere in the stomach, and somehow the idea of a bullet inside him was far worse than the pain, which wasn't yet all that bad. He tried to avoid the blow, but Snapshot brought the rifle down hard and Farris could only watch it pass his eye and strike his right shoulder. A faintness overtook him, though he felt singularly calm. He was going to kill this man. It was just a matter of retrieving the sickle, which was now on the floor somewhere, probably beneath the table. Above him the man's legs moved away, but by reaching out Farris grabbed and held one of them. It would be foolish to lose now, and the blows punishing his back and shoulders could be endured a little longer.

The sickle felt clumsy in his left hand, yet steady enough when he swung it upward. To his great satisfaction the curved blade missed the broad belt buckle and pierced the man's stomach. Snapshot grunted and looked down in awe at the ridiculous tool embedded within him. Leaning against the table, he began a staggering walk around the kitchen, holding on to the wall with one hand like a drunk. Under the table, Farris watched the man's idiotic, shuffling pilgrimage. The front of his trousers was stained dark and the blood seeped from his pants' legs onto the floor. Near the door he sank to his knees like a man in prayer and vomited. He tried to get up, but, on hands and knees, could only stare dully at the blood and vomitus below him. Farris crawled toward the kneeling figure and, when he reached him, leaned across his back. The man's arms trembled as he strove against Farris's weight, now bearing home the blade. Another stream of blood poured from the man's mouth as he sank to his forearms and arched his back. Farris bore down harder and waited, counting slowly until he thought he reached thirty. Snapshot's neck was unclean, and so too was the coarse yellow hair knotted at the back with rubber bands. When Farris got off the man and looked down, he saw only an eye open and dumbfounded.

He got to his feet with difficulty. Somebody on the radio was talking about winter tires. Light-headed now and nauseated, Farris craved fresh air and moved toward the door, holding his left arm across his stomach, afraid to look down at his wound. When he opened the door, the poodle, shivering with cold, wriggled past his legs. The absurd little animal stepped around the fallen man with precise, tiny steps and sniffed the floor. Then he went to a corner by an old stove and sat looking up at Farris.

On the veranda Farris sat down on the musty, damp sofa and stared out at the snow falling thickly through the yellow light overhead. He had lost his watch, but he guessed it wasn't yet nine o'clock. Bill Langford would now be watching the hockey game. How the old man used to enjoy it when Farris watched a game with him and told stories about various players. That one was in trouble with loan sharks. Another had boyfriends in certain cities he visited. Farris wondered also about Madeline Greene and whether her party was still going on. And Mrs. Farnsworth, who would now be in Portugal with her husband. He tried not to think of his wife and her lover in some hotel room overlooking the sea. Perhaps they had now finished dinner and were preparing for bed.

The Doberman had dragged itself toward the house and now lay twenty feet from the veranda. The writer watched as the dog flopped arkly in the snow like some great landed fish. And Farris thought, too, of Jonathan, now lying in the earth of St. James Cemetery. He wondered if snow was also falling on the cold grass above his son. Farris would have enjoyed a drink and there was whiskey in the Volkswagen. But that seemed an impossibly far way off, and he felt too tired. It was all he could do to keep his remaining eye open. And then, after a while, he couldn't do even that.